UNDER THE SOUTHERN CROSS

DAVID MILLER

UNDER THE SOUTHERN CROSS

A NOVEL

David Miller 2020

'There is no flag large enough to cover the shame of killing innocent people'

Voltaire 1694-1778

'He avoided fixed battles with Hannibal and attacked his extended supply lines reckoning that time was on his side in the battle'

Quintus Fabius Maximus 213 BC

Cover : Charles Neville Blaker and his pals from the South African 'Rough Riders' see Chapter 9

SYNOPSIS

In 1899 the Boer War began post the discovery of Diamonds near Kimberley on the Vaal River and also near that time the worlds biggest Gold reserves near Witwatersrand and a subsequent refusal by the Governments of the Orange Free State and Transvaal to grant franchise to the miners who flocked in to the two Boer states.

In total there will be over 450,000 Empire troops battling the Boer farmers in frontal attacks and conventional warfare until the approx. 40,000 Boers , completely outnumbered and with limited resources resort to Guerilla warfare, an area in which they excel and which will extend the conflict for nearly another two years after the ceding of the two states to the British forces.

Louis Badenhorst has killed his first Lion when he was 9 years old and later in life leaves his farm with his neighbour to join the Boer rebels and experiences the fighting and ultimate surrender in 1902. He takes up a new vocation as a big game guide and takes as his first client Bill Gibson a New Zealander who has elected to stay on, post the war, to obtain some trophies to take back to his family home and until recently has been an enemy of the Boer.

In a final reconciliation Louis and Bill have recognised a common disillusionment with the conflict and face a dramatic conclusion in the continued quest for gold by other parties throughout the story and the final conclusion may shock you but bring to closer to a concept of what war is really about and who wins at the end of hostilities!

Learn about the British Concentration Camps which changed the face of warfare to come and were later used by Hitler as a model for the WW 2 Camps ; of the post war social reforms introduced to Britain by Baden-Powell and others as a result of the poor conditions of the population and life in the slums of London ; of the daring escape by the war correspondent Winston Churchill ; of the actions of Lord Roberts and Kitchener and the 'scorched earth' policy later used in the Vietnam conflict ; Kruger and other historical figures through out the novel and the machinations which took place during parts of the conflict and the aspirations of the Colonial Forces and Countries who sought a recognition within the British Empire.

I am indebted to those friends who viewed and commented on sections of the book , to Wikipedia which I used to confirm many of my recalls regarding the history of the event (I made a donation in recognition) to David Blaker of South Africa and now New Zealand for his valuable comments and criticism of the work , the photographs of the environment in which the war was fought in the later stages and for the excerpts and photographs from his Grandfathers Diary (a member of the 'Rough Riders' in the conflict) sections of his diary have been used with permission in the Chapter 9 English South African Residents in the conflict.

ORANGE FREE STATE (1899)
Only some roads/rails shown   Not to Scale

David Miller 2020

TRANSVAAL (1899)

Only some roads/rails shown   Not to Scale

David Miller 2020

UNDER THE SOUTHERN CROSS

INDEX

GLOSSARY

Terms and Characters

Afrikaans	The language of the Afrikaners
Afrikaner	A Boer predominantly of Dutch descent
Arthur Conan Doyle	Newspaper Correspondent a contemporary of Churchill and author of Sherlock Holmes
Baden -Powell	The key figure involved in the siege of Mafeking and the founder of the Scouts movement post war as a response to the poor physical condition of many English youth.
Boer Boere (plural)	A farmer/s (from the Orange Free State or Transvaal) often a mix of Dutch, Huguenot French, German and others
Churchill (Winston)	Already famous and a journalist turned war correspondent who famously escaped from capture by the Boers. Continued fame throughout the next two World Wars. Also Politician and writer / artist. His Aunt Lady Sarah Wilson (nee Churchill) was recruited to be one of the first woman war correspondents during the Siege of Mafeking.
Donga	A dry watercourse or deep depression in the ground.
Field Pieces	A generic term for artillery including cannon, machine guns, mortars etc. the Boer had significant quantities as the war begun but gradually reduced and became less important as guerrilla warfare intensified
Fontein	Fountain, well or spring a suffix to many place names adjacent to these water sources eg. Elandsfontein
Gembok	A South African Oryx - alternative name
Great Trek (the)	The Trek undertaken by the Boer from British rule seeking new homelands to the North and the founders of Orange Free State and Transvaal
Kaffir	A very derogatory name for a black African (from Arabic for 'unbeliever' (Kafir or Kefir)
Kipling (Rudyard)	Newspaper correspondent a contemporary of Churchill and author of 'The Jungle Book', 'Kim' and other works. The animal characters in 'The Jungle Book' were later used as names for the Cub movement Instructors.
Kitchener	British Commander after Roberts, famous as the face and finger on the WW1 posters 'your country needs you'

Kopje / Koppie	A hill usually flat topped (Kop = Hill)
Kraal	A native building or village
Ladysmith	A significant siege of this town by the Boers which lasted 118days ; Winston Churchill rode in with the first relief column.
Mafeking	Town famous for the siege by the Boers which lasted 217 days, made Baden- Powell famous and had many significant public celebrities effectively imprisoned during the siege.
Orange Free State	The area bounded by the Orange River and the Vaal River, originally called Orange River Sovereignty by the British and now the Free State Province.
Roberts	British Commander until Orange Free State and Transvaal ceded to British in 1900 when he left for India assuming the war had finished.
Stoep	Verandah in Afrikaans
Transvaal	Area as named South African Republic by Boers and Transvaal (across the Vaal) by British
Uitlander – Outlander	A foreign migrant worker in the Witwatersand Gold Rush.
Vaal	The River between Orange Free State and Transvaal.
Veldt	Plains often many miles wide and flat appearing featureless
Veldt (the High)	In the North the High Veldt are plains but at an elevation sometimes near 5000 feet *(this is the area in which English troops were said to have frozen to death on guard duty)*

Chapter 1/ The Boer War

Obscene ways to Die

June 4th 1902

My Dearest Mary

At last the war is over and ended 31st May.

We are now just doing a final mopping up , tidying our gear and mounts for the final times and undergoing the final resolution with our former enemies.

Bill and I have been lucky , as you will know several of our mates have paid the ultimate price over here and others will bring home the scars of wars , where we are both unscathed .

This is a beautiful country and there are plenty of opportunities , several of our mates have elected to stay on as Constabulary which means their four shillings a day instantly goes to the equivalent sixteen shillings a day.

As you know I intend to stay as well and we should discuss our future together , I can see us living here permanently and I am so happy you see it the same way , you could bring your Mother too if she agrees and we could enjoy a lifestyle we would only dream of in New Zealand. Land is going to be made available to deserving people to re establish farms in this beautiful country , an opportunity I am unlikely to ever get in New Zealand.

You can almost start to book your fares and I can tell you all about where we can live and all the other stuff when I get the details.

All my love

James

The Boer War has been over for 4 days now; on the 31st May the 'Treaty of Vereeniging' was signed and the Boers relinquished control of their country to the British forces.

At one of the 4000 or so Blockhouses built during the course of the War, across the Orange Free State and Transvaal, Sergeant Brockman of the British forces has despatched the 6 New Zealand infantry, from near Wonderfontein in Transvaal, to patrol an area approx. 20 miles to the North making contact with such Boer Kommando's as they encounter and return with them to the blockhouse on the morrow to surrender their arms and have their details recorded for the military records before they are released to return to their properties.

They are under the nominal command of Corporal Rex Smith and although each of the 6 has a horse they are not regarded as Cavalry and they will alternately lead and ride their mounts. 20 miles will take them at least a day and they will have to bivouac overnight before returning with, or without, any Boer they have encountered or not.

The New Zealanders volunteered for the War to protect the British Empire, and their Queen Victoria who has sadly passed away during the term of the conflict, and for the Honour of New Zealand; secretly an underlying reason for some of them was the 'boys own adventure' in a foreign land and in a 'gentleman's war'.

The sun is beating down and the day is hot, there is a heat shimmer in the distance over the grasses of the open veldt , to their right and a few hundred metres distant is a small hill (or Kopje as they are called here) – perhaps five hundred metres across the base and about fifty metres high and beyond that, and perhaps another two or three kilometres distant, the mountain ranges and rocky slopes are sighted.

After travelling perhaps 15 miles they sight the remains of one of the Boer farms spread across the ground, thrown about in disarray,obviously post the dynamiting of some of the farm buildings .

James Merritt is leading and continues past for about another fifty metres and veers towards the Kopje seeking the slight elevation which will allow them to view more country, so far they haven't encountered any Boers and the day is beginning to wear, the hot sun and lack of shade, the poisoned water wells and the bleak featureless country is beginning to tire them and they are looking forward to preparing their Bivouac shortly and to rest up the animals and themselves.

James is on foot leading his mount and passes a heap of rubble from the old farm buildings consisting of several stones in a heap, he glances towards the Kopje and see several more similar heaps aligned across the plain and suddenly realises what he is looking at .

Wilhelm is lying on the ground near the top of the Kopje, his Mauser rifle is resting atop his rolled up blanket, he has been waiting for the 'Khaki' to reach the 500 metre heap of stones, as he sees him align to the mark he breathes in, holds his breath, and slowly squeezes the trigger.

As soon as he has fired, he sees the 'Khaki' fall and sprints to his mount waiting on the far side and dashes away from the area, lashing at his mount to get as far away, as fast as he can.

James' head is punched sideways, the retort of the rifle sounds a millisecond later, and he slumps to the ground, the men of the patrol begin firing towards the Kopje, while Bill rushes to the aid of James.

The British had come up with the idea of a 'dum dum' bullet early in the conflict and had supplied British Mk IV hollow nosed bullets to maximise injuries, although they were contrary to International conventions. The Boers have not had access to these types of projectile but have made their own semblance of a 'dum dum' by cutting a cross in the lead centre nose of their bullets and it is one of these that has hit James.

The projectile at a residual velocity still over seven hundred metres a second has struck the lower mandible of James' jaw, as it has begun to tumble it has also expanded to near ten times its original diameter, it has travelled almost parallel to his jawbone destroying it completely and then 'ripped out his tongue as it has blown away the whole lower side of his face and jaw and has also taken a section of his throat and neck before exiting.

The horribly disfigured face the gaping throat and exposed windpipe and terrible rasping breaths plus the blood spilling onto the ground horrify Bill and he desperately begins to reach for a cloth to try and staunch the wound .

Bill sees the staring , shocked eyes staring at him, the shaking head as if somehow James can put himself together again; the horrific injury and the suffering make Bill turn to the side and suddenly he is vomiting uncontrollably on the ground retching in anguish and shame that he can't think what to do !

The others have stopped firing , they see the Boer escape over the Kopje, and gather around the writhing figure, the shocking injury sickens them all, they are horrified and helpless – what do you do in a situation like this ?

Rex walks over, lifts his rifle puts the barrel against and fires at James head, shards of bone and pieces of hair and brain, despoil the sand .

'You fuckin swine' Bill screams 'what did you do that for, we might have been able to save him, my best mate gone'

'I wouldn't let a dog suffer like that and he was going to die anyway, look at the poor Bastard' Rex retorted, 'someone had to do it and you were busy puking your guts out, if you were any sort of mate you would have done it first'

The others stand staring at the two men, horrified and waiting to see what is going to happen next.

'You four split up into pairs and chase the Boer cowardly bastard, I don't want him back here alive, and you Bill, and I, are going to bury him, then prepare a Bivouac and we are all leaving here in the morning to return to the Blockhouse. Stop your blubbing like a baby, be a man, get to digging a hole and hurry up'

'We are nearly home, James isn't coming with us but that's the 'luck of the draw', we can't change what just happened. For fucks sake stop your blubbing and move'.

Bill is sobbing but nods his head in agreement and begins the grim task. 'Get his tag and personal effects' Rex orders.

Bill removes James service disc, his name, service number, religion and unit are the last record of his life, in his pockets Rex collects a sealed letter to Mary, which he obviously hasn't got around to posting and his canvas wallet with a few shillings and photos of his parents and Mary.

In a short time a depression has been formed in the ground using their trenching shovels and James is rolled into the shallow grave.

'Well what do you want to say ?' Rex asks.

'The lord is my shepherd, I shall not want, in pastures green he lays me down by the still waters, though I walk in the valley of death I fear no evil, goodbye mate, god bless and keep you now, I shan't forget you' Bill intones, wondering to himself if they are even the right words, and with his voice choking during the discourse.

They fill the grave and collect scattered stones to mark the burial spot and to protect the site from Hyenas and other animals, Bill finds a couple of sticks and ties a rudimentary cross and they leave, walking towards the Kopje to set up the Bivouac for the night and await the return of the others.

Rex turns to Bill 'I will tell them all tonight but I am telling you now pull yourself together and get on with it, if you breathe a sigh of this to anyone I will do you, understand ?'Bill nods and they walk on.

The four other lads have split into two groups and ridden at pace but constantly swerving to minimise the chances of being shot, they have to assume there was only one man as there was only a single shot and they had seen him scrambling over the Kopje .

They know that its almost impossible to shoot a man on a moving horse at long distance or even close quarters, their mounts scramble and stumble as they go up the sides of the slopes, dodging the loose boulders and small scrub and trees as they go. Its only a small hill and as they round the slope they see the dust in the distance and Wilhelm low over the saddle and spurring away.

The pursuit begins from each side, its simple to follow him by the dust rising as Wilhelm continues across the veldt, he is desperate to reach the safety of the hills in the distance where he will be able to lose his pursuers in the rocks and canyons of the range but his horse is already beginning to tire .

Neither he, nor the horse, have had water since the day before and they are both beginning to flag 'maybe I should have waited for the others, and carried on with my scouting, instead of waging my one man war' he thought to himself 'too late now I have made my choice, its some revenge for Marie and the children and I hope they are at peace'

Suddenly his horse slows and begins to whinny and limp, he has thrown a shoe and the stones of the veldt have caused a penetration wound deep in the frog on his foreleg, in minutes he has come to a complete stop, head down and in obvious distress. Wilhelm dismounts and sees that the wound is beginning to bleed and he knows the mount is not going to recover from this; with a sad heart, for the horse has been a good companion to him, he removes his saddle and accoutrements 'one good thing , there isn't much to take off now', he thinks recalling when he had set off from his home over a year ago laden with ammunition, arms and equipment.

He lays them out on the ground and raises his rifle and puts an end to the horses suffering with a shot to the brain .

He turns and sees the riders coming from each side 'I have no chance against four, and on foot, but I have one last chance to take a couple more with Gods help' he thinks and he lays his rifle against the saddle and raises his hands in the air. 'oorgawe – I surrender' he begins to call out as they near.

He would wave a white flag he thinks ruefully but he hasn't got anything even resembling a white cloth, he is clad in a pair of shorts which are ripped and torn and his tunic is a piece of animal hide which was never properly cured and smells rank even to him, he wears a bowler hat he had procured through the year which is in as bad a condition as the rest of him and he presents a poor specimen.

'Move away from the rifle' calls one of them as they approach to within about fifteen metres from one side, his partner has swung out slightly distant from him and the other two riders are approaching from his rear .

Suddenly he pivots and drops to pick up the rifle, the blast from the shotgun of the second rider as he does so, flings him to the ground .

Wlihelm clutches at his abdomen, the buckshot has torn a great hole, blood is coursing out through his fingers which are desperately trying to hold his intestines in and he is rapidly beginning to weaken.

The troops have dismounted.

'You stupid bastard, the war has been over for four days and we were just going to take you to a place of surrender, but you put paid to that and now you are going to die' says one of the soldiers.

'Please help me' Wilhelm begs.

'We aren't going to help you by wasting another bullet, die by yourself, you don't need our help' was the response as they all gathered around the now trembling form, shuddering in the all consuming pain.

Wilhelm looked to the sky 'my God , take me to join my family' he mouthed as the others watched on , 'water' he rasped.

'Drink on this , you bastard' they said as they began to unbutton their flys and urinate on him 'our last gift to you , go and join your other heathen mates' were their final words as he lost consciousness and then his life.

'Leave him to the animals, its all he deserves' one of them said as they remounted and began to ride back to the Kopje 'I hope there aren't any more like him around, and if there are I hope we don't met them, it's a poor reward for James' death but it is some revenge.'

June 6th

Pretoria South Africa

Dear Mr and Mrs Merritt

I am so sorry with the recent loss of your Son James

As I was present when he was killed my Sergeant has asked that I write this missive to you.

James was tragically killed after the cessation of hostilities by a Boer sniper continuing their practice of a cowardly war and striking from cover then retreating as fast as they can.

I can advise you , which may afford you some slight solace , that we issued swift retribution to the Boer for your sons death and he has paid with his own life.

I can say that James was well liked and died instantly from the cowards shot , so he did not suffer at all , which may be some small consolation.

James was interred with a Christian burial attended by his fellows and prayers were offered for his salvation .

I trust this is of some comfort in your sad loss.

Signed   Rex Smith   Corporal NZ Army 2457

For Sergeant William Campbell

June 6th

Pretoria South Africa

Dear Mr and Mrs Merritt,

I am sure you will know by now of James' death at the hands of a Boer Sniper

What terrible luck as the War had ended 4 days before and we were just engaged on 'mopping up' operations

As you know James and I enlisted on the same day and he became my best mate through thick and thin both before we left and since in South Africa and I was to be Best Man at his forthcoming marriage to his betrothed Mary.

I know that relations had become strained in some regards but I am sure that you still deeply loved your son as I did and will mourn his passing

I enclose some of his effects which I recovered for you, may they bring you some memory of your son and my great friend

My sincere condolences and regards

I remain

Bill (William) Gibson

Chapter 2 : The Protagonists – 'for South Africa'

Represented by President Paul Kruger

Pretoria 21ˢᵗ May 1900

Paul Kruger was reflecting on his life to date .

Paul or 'Oom Paul' (Uncle Paul) as he was known by his idolising population was a big man, bearded and of a strong stature. He was a devout believer in the doctrine and beliefs of the fundamentalist religion of the Dutch Reformed Church, a religion almost unique to the Boers and one which regarded life as a constant sacrifice and striving towards a reverence for the Lord.

He had been the President of the South African Republic, or Transvaal as it was also known, since 1883 which was a long time in the history of his country and had also been a time of great changes.

He had a rigid belief in the words of the Bible and the Hymns of his religion brought a calming of his sometimes vociferous arguments with non adherents, he could recall Joshua Slocum visiting during his voyage around the world in the boat the 'Spray' and correcting him when he dared to suggest he was sailing around the World and advising him he was only sailing about the World, which of course was flat !

His wife Gezina had borne 16 children and 'praise the Lord' 9 had survived although 7 had died either in childbirth or shortly after 'God indeed placed troubles upon us but there is a divine reason behind everything on earth' he mused.

His life seemed to have been one struggle after another and could be considered almost a condensation and summary of the Boer history.

From the Great Trek to establish their homes in what was later recognised by the British as the South African Republic and the Orange Free State, to the battles with the Zulu, their later battles with the Zulu in conjunction with the British and the subsequent vanquish of the native tribes and to the first Boer War of 1880-1881, Kruger remembered them all.

The South African Republic and the Orange Free State had finally gained recognition, the Orange Free State at the treaty of Sand river in 1852 and the South African Republic at Bloemfontein in 1854, although the British called the South African Republic the Transvaal (meaning across the Vaal River the boundary between the two states.)

He remembered the first Boer War and how he had negotiated the British overtures for peace after their various defeats , he recalled with pride the surrender of the British at O'Neills cottage in March 1881 and how proudly he had seen his parliament endorse and complete the process .

The most telling defeat for the British, and possibly the final act for them, had been the battle for Majuba where the Boers' Webley Richards rifles and the marksmanship of the Boer soldiers, unmatched by the British who had only been trained to fire in volleys with little actual aiming, had resulted in a massive Boer victory .

At the end of the battle the statistics made grim reading for the British with 92 dead, 131 injured and 53 taken prisoner for the loss by the Boer forces of 1 dead and 6 injured, an example of how good marksmanship and skills in the difficult country could work to advantage against superior numerical forces .

He had seen this latest war coming for a long time now.

When Diamonds had been found near the Vaal River in 1867 and after the huge influx of Uitlanders (outsiders) from Britain and around the world had taken place , and then to be repeated again with the discovery of the Worlds biggest Gold ore reserves near Witwatersrand in 1886 he had warned ' Trouble is going to follow these discoveries and no good will come of it, our country will be soaked in blood'

How he had been proved right; from the failed coup by Cecil Rhodes in 1896 to the present, the British were always going to want control of the States they had once ceded and the current war had been almost inevitable, Gold was the underlying reason for the war although the British cited the refusal to grant the vote to the outsiders (Uitlanders) as the main reason for the conflict adding their concerns regarding the Boers continuing to keep slaves.

 For the first part of this latest war it appeared the Boer were again going to win for similar reasons to the first added to the fact they had now been armed with considerable resources of men, rifles and horses and plus a large number of field pieces supplied by German East Africa, who had no more love of the British than the Boers, however their early strategy of attacking and blockading the British forts had been a failure and Kruger was now being forced to realize the battle was nearly lost.

Although there had been support from around the World, and some Americans had joined the battle on the Boer side plus arms and munitions were being supplied by German East Africa he was aware that American and other industries and countries were taking advantage of being able to sell and supply to the British vast amounts of resources, without the necessity of having to breach the British Navy blockade of the Boer strongholds.

The British had been supported by a vast increase in the size of their force supplemented by troops from throughout the Empire and now had nearly four hundred thousand against a severely depleted Boer force now reduced to about thirty thousand or so and the end seemed imminent with the vast disparity now.

Paul had been in discussions with Martinus Steyn, the President of the Orange Free State who had been forced to retire to the relative safety of Pretoria and on this day they were discussing their strategy for the future, with them were their assembled Generals, Christiaan Botha , Schalk Burger, Christian de Wet, Jacobus Joubert, Louis Botha and Piet Cronje with his field General Koos de la Rey, they had all travelled by train where possible or horse and cart and were accompanied by several officers and men assembled with various horses, mules, oxen and wagons.

'We don't have much time, the British troops are at our gates and threatening to take our beloved Pretoria and are only a few days from annexing our Orange Free State, do we sue for peace' Paul asked 'I am going to take a vote, you will all have discussed this between yourselves and with each other, for myself I think we have to reconcile to the fact our cause is lost' he added .

'Those who vote for seeking a settlement with the British now place your tick on a piece of paper, I will abstain but will count your votes, thank you, vote now'

'Well I am surprised' he said a couple of minutes later 'and so very proud of you , the vote is unanimous to continue the fight , I guess we have done it before in the last war with unequal forces but there are a lot more Colonial troops this time and I must confess they seem to be more of a handful than the Brits'

Christian Botha spoke 'We think you should both seek asylum out of Pretoria and the Transvaal, we will be considerably weakened and our troops morale will be put to the test if we let you be captured, we can arrange for people to look after your wife and family in your absence and you will be better utilised pleading our case on the world stage, you are not young men anymore and one of us can act as President until your return, in fact dare I suggest the post is somewhat redundant right at this time!'

Readers Note ; Although the intention to send the two Presidents to safety was intended in good faith Pauls Wife and his Grandchildren were interned in a British Concentration camp after he had left them behind , six of the nine grandchildren were dead within a week and his wife died two days after them. Back to the story !

Paul and Martinus reluctantly agreed that capture could demoralise the Boer forces and that they would try to get more World support for their cause.

'We will make arrangements to leave in about three months or so , by then we will have a better idea of how things are developing , if we are to continue we need continued access to the armaments and ammunition and supplies from German East Africa and we will have to pay for them' Paul said 'we have most of our Gold Reserves and also have all of the precious metals and Diamonds from our Pretoria Mint ; I will take a quantity with me but the rest of the bullion must be shared among you so that you can continue your individual battles and have a resource available to re arm as you need to , I suggest we divide our financial resource into 7 lots and you each take your share and hide it where you can and so you can readily access it when you need it' he added.

'It is vital it doesn't fall into the hands of our enemy , there will be almost 50,000 pounds and about ten gold ingots each and you must ensure only your most trusted men know of the locations when you hide it away – I myself will load a freight wagon with our share of the funds stowed below stores of Iron and Timber and I am sending it to Mozambique as soon as it is ready, our agent in the area is going to lodge it in the Portuguese Bank under an assumed name and identity until I arrive'

'Can we discuss now, your intentions for the future and lets see what resources we actually have at present' he suggested.

Piet Joubert was first to answer followed by the others , in total they had nearly twenty five thousand soldiers, near one hundred and forty field pieces of which de Wet seemed to have the biggest amount, forty thousand Mauser rifles and pistols (of which some ten thousand were still stored in oilcloth) and over thirty five thousand Horses, Oxen and Mules .

'On the basis of some of our earlier successes that should prove a handful for the Brits if we continue our guerrilla warfare, strike at their trains with explosives and field pieces and shoot

from a distance then retire to the safety of the mountains where they are at a disadvantage'
was the consensus of opinion, they were each to set off in differing directions but to meet and
discuss common strategies and concerns as the war continued and assuming they were able '
it is important we break out of the British drives , we will be powerless against the
blockhouses and barbed wire if we are forced towards them , the last one by our intelligence
suggested there are nearly fifty thousand troops beginning to mass and preparing to begin a
'drive' against us towards their barbed wire and Blockhouses in one major action, let them
encircle and drive no one, we must escape at all costs wherever we can and fight again
elsewhere, they will soon get tired of that we just have to continue to be smarter' commented
de Wet.

Easier said than done ! Although most of the armies have evaded and escaped the great
drive by February the next year de Wet will have lost all his field guns near the Caledon
River and will be in full retreat pursued by Kitcheners force, Cronje plus his Five thousand
Boers will have been defeated near Paardeberg and none of the others will be doing much
better, but for the moment there is a shared confidence that they can still win out.

Within a few months Roberts has assembled a force of near twenty thousand troops and is
determined to encircle and capture the 2 Presidents, his force is met by Five thousand Boers
under Botha at the 'Battle of Burgendahl' over the period 21-27 August and the Boers are
overwhelmed (so much for fighting from cover) their defensive strategy is in tatters and they
are in rapid disbursement and retreat as the British forces march into Machadorp and
consolidate their position establishing new concentration and POW camps and sending out
roving patrols to seek out remnants of Botha's troops.

By late August the Kruger Gold reserves have been despatched to Mozambique and Paul and
Martinus are now moving East towards Barberton and are being pursued by the Empire
forces. The capture of the two Presidents would be a severe blow to Boer morale and a great
coup for the British Generals, who are by now being mocked by some of the Press for their
inability to do just that.

On the 11th September 1900 they finally left the Transvaal by train towards Mozambique and
the port of Laurenco Marques, Paul wept as they crossed the border to safety and forced to
leave his beloved home.

On arrival they met a guard of the Portuguese Governor who took them to, and directed them
to stay, in a local hotel . They had arranged and intended to board the German East Africa
Line ship the 'Herzog' however, the British Consul had arranged with the Portuguese to place
them under house arrest and the vessel sailed without them.

'You have no right to imprison us like this, by what right? Are you puppets of the British
Government?' Paul ranted but to no avail, the Governor was resolute and frantically trying to
ascertain his governments official policy in this regard, while staving off British overtures to
release the two prisoners to a British Command and return them to South Africa.

The Kruger Gold reserves still sat in a wagon in a shed hidden from prying eyes and guarded
by sympathisers of the Boer cause.

It is a month later when Queen Wilhemina of the Netherlands has made a deal with Britain to
release the prisoners and allow them to be carried to refuge on the continent and safe passage

through the British blockade. Accordingly the Dutch warship HNLMS 'Gelderland' arrives to uplift the passengers and their belongings, the Gold reserves are loaded aboard the vessel and the Captain welcomes his distinguished guests on board.

A crowd of sympathisers to the Boer cause crowd the wharf and cheer as the vessel begins to leave the wharf waving flags and cheering 'god speed and good luck'.

And so the first share of the Kruger gold reserves leaves the African continent 'I do wonder that our Generals have been able to protect and use the other reserves to continue their battle against the British' Paul mused.

Readers Note: The Gelderland landed the two Presidents at Marseille, to a rapturous welcome of over sixty thousand people, many throughout the world applauded the courageous Boer stand against the British and supported their cause, there was an official reception in Paris and then Cologne, however, Kaiser Wilhelm refused to meet them in Berlin and Paul was deeply shocked 'The Kaiser has betrayed us' he said to Martinus.

Paul never returned to his beloved country although Martinus did in later years and Paul continued to try to seek world support to his cause to little effect and within a couple of years he was living in Utrecht in Holland and latterly in Western Switzerland, partially blind and totally deaf until his death in 1904.

After the war many of the Boer Generals toured the world and were rapturously received by great throngs of people and huge applause and acclamation; astoundingly this was also the practice in England and Britain. This was a recognition of the Boer solidarity and bravery resisting a hugely more powerful force which at the end of the war had seen approximately fifty thousand Boers resist the Empire forces in total of over four hundred and fifty thousand for over three years.

The British Concentration camps had introduced a new dimension to war when in excess of sixty percent of all children interred had died, together with the high numbers of women that also succumbed and for the first time more non combatants had died than soldiers.

The practice of erecting memorials to the war dead began in earnest after the Boer War in Britain, although there had been a few relating to the Crimea war, most of the Boer War memorials fell into disrepair or were removed in the twentieth century as an unintended consequence of a post Imperial guilt.

Chapter 3 : The Protagonists - 'for the British Empire'

Lord Kitchener

Military Headquarters British Forces

November 30ᵗʰ 1900

'Good morning Gentleman of the general Staff and others' Kitchener began , 'we can cheer today another hard fought victory at Rhenoster Kop yesterday, however , it is time for a new strategy and an end to this war'

Kitchener has just been appointed commander of the Empire forces following the departure of Lord Roberts to his new role as Viceroy to India, a post he has been waiting impatiently to fill; with the ceding of Orange Free State and now the Transvaal he considers the war effectively over and he can leave Kitchener to attend on the final tidying up.

Kitchener continued 'We need one final push to bring the war to a conclusion, and there are several policies that will bring it to that end as follows:'

'We are going to initiate a 'scorched earth policy'; for too long the Boers have continued to provision and use mounts plus the refuge of some of their homes, this is going to end, the general directive to all farms in the Transvaal and Orange Free State requiring them to complete an 'Oath of Allegiance' to the Queen' is obsolete, it has not worked and been breached constantly anyway and we will withdraw that opportunity for protection as soon as possible.'

'The occupants of those farms will be stripped of all their resources, this includes all stock, crops and materials we can use, everything else is to be destroyed and rendered useless, if the only recourse is to poison wells if they can't be plugged, so be it, we will leave nothing to aid the rebels'

'Women and children are to be moved to the nearest railhead and put on trains to our concentration camps, we are going to expand on Lord Roberts initiatives in this respect, I have been advised we may have to incarcerate up to 125,000 women and children and this will require at least 36 camps at current levels or another 16 to be built starting straight away, if we can get an early surrender this can all come to a halt'

'The Boers won't enjoy seeing their families in the camps and I can't see them sticking it out much longer especially in conjunction with my 'scorched earth' policy'

'America has promised us horses up to a possible 100,000 plus 50,000 mules , we already have made inroads into those figures, but we are still losing horses, oxen and mules at an alarming rate so we will have to monitor this carefully and ensure we keep up sufficient for our purposes'

'I think that's all. I am going to discuss the details with my Generals and they will begin after this meeting to implement my new policy, the end is in sight we just have to be resolute and it will be over in short shrift'

'I must say I like having the whole thing cut and dried and worked out – lets get to it' and Kitchener glared around the room almost daring anyone to criticise his strategy.

The room emptied except for a number of his Generals who awaited the apportionment of the various responsibilities.

Now that the war was nearly over, and the new strategy was going to ensure that happened in a short while, a lot of the pressure for results was reducing . Kitchener and his staff knew that there was only a handful of rebels left, the formal annexation of the Orange Free State had occurred back on the 28th May and of Transvaal or the South African Republic on 25th October this year.

It was decided that a number of the British troops could be sent home, fresh Colonial troops were continuing to arrive and could be used for the mopping up operations – they had proved to be better horsemen and more suited to the guerrilla type war with roving parties of relatively small forces striking out and self supporting on occasions .

By wars end there will have been over 450,000 Empire forces engaged in the battle nevertheless at this point in time there was a confidence both in the new strategy and a positive outcome in the near future .

'We need to continue our policy of establishing blockhouses and barbed wire entanglements between them and then we will be in a position to drive the rebels towards them with our superior forces and it will be simple to force their surrender or watch them die in their cause!' one of the Generals had opined 'perhaps we can utilise some of the Negro labour force from our Black concentration camps that aren't going to be worked in the mines'

'Excellent thinking' endorsed Kitchener 'we can start that as soon as you can make arrangements, they only need a minimum of looking after and can make their own daub huts to live in, a bit of game to keep them fed, and this will also demonstrate our compassion towards the Blacks and give them something to work for'

'The Blockhouses need to be established concentrated along the Northwest Transvaal and the North boundary of Orange Free State so that they will also give a protection to the Government policy of reopening the Gold and Diamond mines, we have the required workforce in the Blacks we have in their separate concentration camps, and this will assist the Empire to fund the costs that have been imposed as a result of the war' Kitchener added ' a good idea, the Blockhouses and fences are relatively simple to construct, I don't see such a need in the areas to the South – the resources and rebels seem to concentrating in NW Transvaal and most of the important mines are in the area, if we have to we can cross the whole area with a system of linked blockhouses and effectively cut off the rebels' Kitchener supported this initiative. ' this is the type of thinking that will bring the conflict to an early end, I trust you will all act accordingly, the sooner they are complete we can began a policy of 'drives' against the Boers and lets see how they go against our protected machine guns'

Kitchener's war continues, although the rebel Boers are continually striking at his troops and the rail systems and then retreating to the sanctuary of the ravines and mountains where they enjoy the supremacy of their marksmanship and sniping. This is proving a successful strategy for the Boers but means the war must drag on for what seems an interminable time with the British unable to concentrate the Boer forces for a frontal attack and the Boers content to just keep attacking in small lightning raids and then retreating to cover.

The Colonial troops are much better at hunting out the Boer and competing in this environment, and especially the Australians where the dry featureless veldt resembles their 'outback' and the mountains and swamps are also a similar environment to many of their homes, and the British troop numbers are gradually reducing as more and more troops are being sent back to Britain.

The British people are becoming annoyed at the resistance from the Boer and the affront that they dare to resist the Empire forces and a number of homes and shops of people of Dutch or French origins are burnt to the ground in England and the papers are rabid in their criticism of the Boer forces and population.

On 14th May 1901 Kitcheners staff have assembled 50,000 troops to take part in the great trek and force the Boers towards the blockhouses near the Swaziland border and while they are assembled despatch them with machine guns from the fortifications. Unfortunately two battalions are withdrawn from the initial nine and sent to pursue de Wet who has taken his Kommando South and this leaves a gap in the Empire lines, through which most of the Boers escape, and the nett result of the great drive is a miserable 3000 Boer prisoners after months of effort.

In early 1901 Emily Hobhouse had visited the White concentration camps and been horrified at the conditions, she had written '----I call this camp system a wholesale cruelty-----to keep the camps going is murder to the children---' the British Press is scathing in its criticism of her report and labels her a traitor.

'That accursed nosey woman is poking her nose in and looks like she is determined to undermine us in the British Press, I don't want this to reflect badly on our Army so I want the mopping up operations and a large part of the camp policing carried out by Colonial troops – this includes the Canadian , Australians, New Zealanders and Indians – I don't want any trouble and I also don't want to affect our British troops morale, some of these Colonials seem to enjoy this type of stuff so it will serve a dual purpose' Kitchener has decided.

The Author Conan Doyle who is a war correspondent takes a photo of 7 year old Lizzie van Zyl, (who subsequently died on the 9th May 1901,) and quotes her sunken eyes and wasted skeletal body as an example of the poor mothers the Boer women are, and the British Press publishes these pictures and caricatures of gargoyle like monsters and harridans as examples of the low class of the Boers. An early example of demonising the opposing races.

However, some of the returning soldiers are beginning to reinforce the accusations of Emily Hobhouse regrading conditions in the Concentration Camps and questions are starting to be posed in Parliament, finally the Government sends Millicent Fawcett to visit the camps and she agrees and concedes that the comments of Emily Hobhouse are well founded. By this time the mortality rate for children under 16 has soared to near 65% and the Government is forced to act, the administration of the camps is taken over by civilian authorities with an almost immediate improvement in conditions.

(Readers Note: At the wars end there will have been 110,000 women and children interred in 42 camps for Whites and an indeterminate number for Blacks, and near 26,250 dead in the Boer camps of which 22,000 have been children)

Neither of the women viewed the concentration camps established for the Blacks and Kitchener, who has had them incarcerated as well in even worse conditions in some cases, has been using the Black labour to build the blockhouses and barbed wire entanglements and large numbers have been transported to and begun working in the gold and diamond mines which have been reopened.

The 'scorched earth' policy has seen nearly 30,000 farms destroyed, hundreds of Blacks kraals as well as several towns and villages levelled to the ground, and near the end of 1901 although farms are still being destroyed the residents are not being taken to the camps but left to fend for themselves against the vagaries of the weather with no shelter against the elements and wild animals and with a hope that the Boer forces will be forced to defend the families left.

It is the end of 1901 and still the Boer resistance continues, the British public and Press is now starting to question why the war is taking so long to bring to an end and is scathing that the might of the British Empire is being opposed by a few thousand inferior Boer rebels, the British Generals are bereft of new ideas but continue to harass and restrict the Boer movements. Gradually all of the field pieces have been taken and thousands of prisoners have been captured adding to the logistical problems of looking after and feeding so many and the war is getting even more bitter in areas with directives among field staff to 'take no prisoners'

In February 1902 Kitcheners forces are progressing another drive, this time forcing deWet's Kommando in the Orange Free State towards the North and the Vaal River and a number of actions are taking place across the various fields of battle, early overtures for peace have been rejected but on the 31st May 1902 the Boer Generals de Wet, Botha and de la Rey finally sign a peace treaty at Vereeniging and its finally over without the Boers having to fight through another winter and in any event almost exhausted of troops and weapons.

And so it ends with a whimper and although there is a British administration established before long the Afrikaners will be back to controlling their independent Orange Free State and Transvaal within South Africa. The British will pay millions in compensation for the damage inflicted to farms and families that have been mistreated throughout the conflict.

There is huge rejoicing in England however within a short time some of the Boer Generals will be touring America and England to huge crowds celebrating their stoic and brave stand against the immense odds of the Empire.

Chapter 4 : The Combatants –'for New Zealand'

James Merritt

24th November 1900 – Saturday Dunedin NZ

James was a young man, 17 years old, bronzed of complexion and with a lean build and fine features, his strong dark hair set off his brown eyes and he stood near 6 foot tall.

In the weekends he was usually spending his time training and drilling with the Otago Volunteer Forces, however , today he had requested and been given a day off for some part time work. In common with many young men of the time work was hard to find and even more difficult to locate a permanent position so he was forced to undertake any work he could find.

He had been working on the McAllister farm, pulling stumps with the draught horses and clearing the land for planting out with pasture in the Summer for an Autumn growth.

He had started the day at 6 in the morning and it was now 4 in the afternoon, he was covered in grime and dirt and he had rubbed the horses down, stored the swarfingles and tack and let the horses go at the home paddock .

He walked up to the house as McAllister came to the step to meet him 'thanks for your help today James, sorry I can't offer you more work just now but keep in touch son, you are a good worker' and he handed him 2 shillings for the days work .

As McAllister re entered the house James set off for home, on the way he passed Jones' garden, a source of the Jones supply of vegetables they used to supplement their income by selling to the community.

'They wouldn't miss a couple of vegetables, and I am getting a bit sick of this piecemeal work with no security and I deserve better' James thought to himself as he looked about before crossing the fence, grabbing a couple of cabbages , putting them into his sugar bag slinging it over his back and continued homeward .

He passed them to his Mother as he entered the house and began washing up in the basin left for that purpose in the kitchen, 'well that's lovely, did McAllisters give them to you, I hope you thanked them' his Mother said.

James did not reply, he was starting to wonder if taking them had been such a good idea and wondered how he could explain how he had acquired them when there was a knock at the door.

James opened the door to see Hamish Jones glaring at him ' do you think I didn't see you stealing my cabbages, you young no good, I expect you to pay for them right now or I will go to the Constabulary and I want a shilling each for them'

'Please be quiet, I will give you the money, I am so sorry' James began as his Mother came out behind him 'Hello Mr Jones she said, nice to see you, do you have some jobs for James'

Hamish Jones face became apoplectic and he punched the air with his finger 'let him tell you' he turned to James 'give me the money and don't come near my place again'

James reached for his 2 shillings 'a whole days work wasted for 2 cabbages worth a couple of pennies or so, God I do some stupid things' he thought as he handed over the money and Jones stalked away.

'Oh James what will your Father say, don't tell me you stole the cabbages, why?, we are not that poor we have to steal'

He said nothing and crept to his room to begin changing into clean clothes and tidying himself up a bit.

Within a few minutes his father stormed into his room ' you wastrel, good for nothing scoundrel, you bring shame on us, stealing a man's cabbages, whatever possessed you ?, the book says "thou shalt not steal" remember that in future; you will have to decide if you want to make something of your life, obey the Scriptures and the Law and decide what you want to do, you are nearly a Man now, grow up and prove it !' ' You shame us by living in this area, what if any news of this gets out, how are we to hold our heads up?'

James pretended to ignore the message but secretly admitted his Father was right and he had been a fool, he continued dressing, he was late to pick up Mary and take her to the Concert which was to start in a couple of hours time.

He had been courting Mary for almost a year now, they had met when he was at School and in spite of his efforts she had completely ignored him for several years, however, now they had both left School and were working, albeit James as a part time general farm hand and without a permanent position, and Mary in the local General Store, they had begun to see more of each other and had found a companionship and friendship.

James knew he was lucky that Mary had taken a 'shine' to him, she was a delightful lass, well liked in the town, with a pleasant personality and she lived with her Widowed Mother .

Her Blonde hair was tied back into a 'pony tail' and she was of a slight build only 5 foot tall with twinkling Blue eyes and rosy lips that had enchanted many young men in the Town and to James she was the 'pick of the crop' and his future Wife he hoped.

They walked into the Main Street and joined the crowds assembling along the path as the Gun Squad of the Otago Church Lads Brigade marched down the street followed by 3 Corps. of the Dunedin Cadets who were firing salutes of blank ammunition skywards as they paraded down the Street until they came to a halt outside the Dunedin Theatre and the parade members and citizens began to file into the Hall .

Tonight the Show was a production with a cast of over 60 players and musicians and was reputed to be an elaborate affair celebrating the great victory over the Boer forces in South Africa with the 'Relief of Mafeking' on 17th May 1900 and including the hero of the event Commander Baden – Powell .

Before the play started , however, the Dunedin Band played a selection of patriotic tunes with the audience singing the popular war tunes of the day. A crowd favourite was 'The Boys of the Southern Cross' which was being sung with considerable fervour by the assembled audience.

We are the boys of the Southern Cross

Our stars shine on our flags

Emblazoned with the Union Jack

To show we're English lads

which had recently been released and the 'Sons of the Colonies – England in Danger !' James and Mary joined in with gusto, 'how lucky we are to be living in the Empire' James whispered to her .

The play began at the conclusion of the Bands contribution and was set in a Military Hospital with wounded Heroes plus Nurses and Doctors and was a story of love, death, sacrifice and betrayal portrayed on the stage.

The enraptured audience cheered as the actions of our brave forces were recounted and booed as the Boer captive in the play was brought into the Hospital as a display of Christian charity to the enemy, he was portrayed as a snivelling weak specimen of a person, subdued and grovelling to his captors . Finally the production ended to a standing ovation and sustained applause.

The evening ended with a Tableau on stage representing 'Brittania and Her Defenders' to further sustained applause before the Town Mayor ended the show, together with a Major Smith of the Otago Regiment reminding the audience that young men were still required to defeat the Boer uprising and bring peace to South Africa and Glory to our Gracious Queen and her Empire, members of the Volunteer Force or Regulars would be considered.

A rendition of the National Anthem 'God Save our Gracious Queen' moved more than one heart and a rousing cheer ended the Concert.

As they left the Theatre James declared to Mary 'I must do my duty and serve our homeland and the Empire, I am going to enlist on Monday, John my elder brother went with the first contingent and now its my turn'

'The war will soon be over and I must act now, the formal annexation of the two states took place late October and there's only a handful of rebels left, I want to be in the final acts of the war if I can, our troops over there now have to be relieved'.

A tear ran down Mary's cheek 'of course you must go and join those brave souls and bring a final peace, I will write to you while you are away.'

'I am going to tell my Mother and Father tomorrow after Church can I pick you up say at 9:30 and I'll walk you to Church'

'Of course was the prompt reply, what are your parents going to say about your decision to enlist ?'

'I have been told to "straighten up" and that's just what I am going to do, they will just have to face it and accept it' was James response.

They said goodnight after James had walked Mary to her door. ' I do hope you know that I am falling for your charms and hope that you will consider marriage on my return from the war, can I talk to your Mother about my intentions before I leave ?'

'You must know I feel the same way and of course we will tell Mother, I hope she will be pleased and look forward to the day that you return and we can begin to plan a wedding, I assume this is your proposal, and I can confirm I have accepted it' she laughed gaily.

'Will you come to lunch after Church tomorrow' James asked.

James almost flew home, now he had decided his duty and confirmed his intentions to Mary and discovered she felt the same way all was right with his world, he just had to convince his parents the next day.

Sundays were a sober affair in the Walsh household, James' Father was an Elder in the local Presbyterian church and was a dour, miserable man . Religion was the important part of his life and he was determined that the rest of the family would tread a path of righteousness as well, whether they wanted to or not.

The day was dedicated to the church and after the service the family would return home to a Sunday lunch and thence an afternoon of quiet rest and contemplation until the evening meal and then the end of the day. It was a day of rest and no one was to undertake anything to the contrary.

On this day James and Mary had attended the Church where the Minister had based his sermon on sacrifice, quoting at length the sacrifice of Jesus but introducing the glorious heroes of the Boer War who had fallen to date and how their sacrifice was almost Holy and affected us all, it had glorified the Empire and the families who had lost loved ones could seek solace in the fact that no man could do more than they had, nor for a richer cause .

He referred to the Boer as little better than Atheists with their strange religion, their practice of still having Black slaves, their use of a heathen language (Afrikaans) which was a mixture of Dutch, German and French and their refusal to bow to British overtures and accept Queen Victoria as the legitimate ruler of South Africa would bring them the suffering they deserved.

The British spirit and bulldog traits had been personified by the War Correspondent Winston Churchill who after being captured and imprisoned in Pretoria had made a daring escape and evaded capture for eight days, hitching on freight trains and hiding in a mine for 6 days, in spite of the Boer 25 pound reward on his head, (Dead or Alive) and who had reached Portuguese East Africa and safety. This was an example of the heights of bravery and resourcefulness that young men of the Empire could aspire to and was the reason victory was certain.

The British forces would also be victorious as they were led by Generals and Christians who had the power of God on their side, the ability to think through strategy and direct the war to minimise losses and maximise gains, with the might of the Empire behind them the end was eminent and true justice would be dispensed to the evil Boers who had dared to stand against our Queen and the Empire in an affront upon our civilisation.

He concluded his sermon with the words 'It is spoken in Psalms Chapter 149 Verse 7 "We shall execute vengeance upon the heathen and punishments upon the people" our cause is just.

His sermon had been received with heart by the congregation, and many positive comments were made as the parishioners were leaving or waiting outside the Church.

James and Mary had gone to lunch at James families house after the service, and following the clearing up post the meal Mary set off for her home, James, his Mother and Father retired to the Drawing Room where James broached the subject of his intentions in respect of Mary and to enlist the next day .

His Mother burst into tears 'I have lost both my daughters, stillborn, your only Brother John has now left to work in Eltham after he returned and I don't know when we will see him again, and now you want to go and break my heart completely, the War must soon be over, why must you go now ? I am pleased that you wish to become engaged to Mary and I could not be happier in that respect but please reconsider for me your intentions regarding the war'

'Nonsense' his Father replied 'pull yourself together woman. Did you not hear the Minister today and listen to the news that the war is almost done, we must trust in the Lord and commit James to his service and await his return, hopefully as a man. If the Lord decides otherwise, what nobler death could there be than in the service of our Queen and the Empire it is time he took some responsibility and matured, God forbid it ever gets out he has been a thief, the best place for him' He rose to his feet and reluctantly shook his sons hand 'I am happy you have listened to my admonition of yesterday, well I assume you listened, and this is not just some selfish jape of your own. I hope you do your duty and try and restore some pride to us'

'We will discuss your pending engagement upon your return I am sure Mary intends to wait and display decorum, there is no need to rush into it and the wait will only confirm your regard for each other, I must say I am pleased I am with your choice of partner, although I don't know why she should accept you, how did her Mother greet the news ?'

'We intend to tell her this afternoon, I hope she will give permission'

'Good Lord James, it is usual to ask the Parents of the intended Bride for their permission first, you must remember there are conventions and reasons for the way of doing things, it's too late now, you had best leave now and make amends and confirm Marys' Mother has no objection to your pending engagement, why don't you ever think before rushing into things?'

Mary's Mother was delighted with the news 'I had hoped you two might build a future together; good luck with your enlistment, I hope all goes well and we can begin making arrangements when you return' she gave a big kiss to James cheek 'I am so happy , you have made my day'

The next few days would see James selected, he would meet Bill and form a lifetime relationship with him and travel to South Africa for the war but for now all that was in the future as was his life with Mary.

Chapter 5 : The Combatants – 'for New Zealand'

Bill Gibson

25ᵗʰ November 1900

Saturday East Taieri New Zealand

The red projectile flew towards him at nearly forty miles an hour 'hold you nerve' flew through his head as he carefully watched the flight of the ball.

He swung his bat and heard the resounding thwack of the willow on leather as he followed through on the swing and watched the ball race to the boundary.

'Well done Sir' called his Pater, amidst the claps from the other spectators 'my son don't you know' he added proudly.

'If he smites the Boers as well as he can hit a Cricket Ball, they won't last long , and he's off to join up on Monday' he addressed the surrounding audience.

Bill Gibson (his real name was William but he used a shorter version when with his mates) was a striking young man, nearly six feet tall and with a sun bronzed complexion to his clean shaven face. His well defined muscle groups evidenced his fitness and strength and others were impressed with his ready wit and good humour.

On this day he was playing for the East Taieri Cricket Club against a team from Dunedin, some fifteen miles North .

The East Taieri Cricket Club was an old institution having been established for some years and with its own facility at the Recreation Ground.

When not playing cricket Bill would often be found at the Tennis Club which operated from the same venue, having being established in 1883 some years later than the foundation of the Cricket Club, and displaying an obvious talent with a tennis ball as well as his cricketing skills.

While the opposing team was recovering the ball, Bill thought about the Monday to come.

He would be presenting himself to the Enlistment board hopefully to be selected for the New Zealand forces to the Boer War.

'I hope I haven't left it too late, it will be terrible if I miss out on the action by delaying my volunteering' he thought .

With his Paters influence in the Community and Military and his skills with horses and rifles plus his membership of the East Taieri Rifles he was confident of selection.

In a few moments it was back to the Cricket and he applied all his concentration to scoring for his team.

It was a proud moment when after the game and at afternoon tea the club captain rose to speak. 'Once again Bill has showed his mettle and ability and helped us markedly with a fine innings at the bat in our win today, but there is a more important matter and that is his intention to sign up for the war on Monday, and you don't need me to tell which war that is. I know Bill will do the country, province and our town proud and I am sure I speak for you all when we wish him god speed and a successful tour and we look forward to his return. Join me in three cheers for Bill – all the best mate and good luck'

Bill rose to his feet 'Thanks for those sentiments' he replied 'I just hope all goes well and I am accepted, it does sound like it might all be over shortly, but if I can get there and help finish it for our glorious Queen and the Empire I will be happy'.

'Those rebellious Boers need to be taught a lesson in respect and it sounds like they are getting one' he added to a further acclaim from all of his team and mates, 'just maybe I can teach them a bit more'

East Taieri was a thriving rural township , complete with Tennis and Cricket Clubs, a High School and Primary School, two newspapers the Taieri Advocate and the Otago Witness and the Holy Cross College, a Roma Catholic Theological College. And not to be outdone had a significant Presbyterian presence (probably a result of the large numbers of Scots who had settled the area originally) with the new Manse a magnificent two storey building near the Church and which had been built in 1877.

It was also a station for the Taieri Gorge Railway of the Central Otago Rail which led to the vast inland plains via Middlemarch .

Bills' Pater was a leading character in the area, with a large landholding and was a Councillor of the Town, a Captain of the East Taieri rifles (a Volunteer force) and Bill worked on the family farm as a shepherd, general hand and other duties on the basis his Pater had explained 'you may be in line to inherit the property but you must first learn the business from the ground up as I did before you'

Bills father or Pater had been one of the 'landed gentry' influential in the introduction of game to New Zealand to create the sportsmans paradise they were intending and had been a founding member in the local Acclimatisation Society. In common with other areas in the new country there had been an explosion of such societies intent on stocking their country with a variety of hunting and shooting resources and in to a land bereft of native mammals they had introduced, generally from England but also other countries, about ten species of Deer including Red, Sika, Fallow and even Moose near Hokitika, Opossums, Wallabies and Kangaroos from Australia, small animals including Hedgehogs, Rabbits, Weasels and Stoats Hares and other creatures and dozens of species of birds which included Ducks, Pheasants, Quail, Chukar, Sparrows, Swans and Hawks and a multitude of others.

These were all, with a few exceptions including the Moose and Kangaroos, thriving in their new environment with no natural enemies or predators and the land was indeed becoming a sporting paradise 'mark my words' his Father had told Bill 'this is to be a more egalitarian society than the old country we have left and with these introductions it won't be long until everyone will be able to provide food and trophies for their families'

At this time however Deer were the preserve of a wealthy few and hunting was restricted to ballot holders who were allowed one stag per year, in spite of his assurances regarding the egalitarian nature of the country Bill suspected that much of the resource was actually still going to be restricted to a privileged few and his Father was always able to obtain a permit each for himself and Bill in the few ballots to date, Bill was too scared to venture that perhaps his Fathers position, money and status had influenced the selection process but happily accompanied him each year, from the age of 12 years, usually by train to the Rakaia area and thence by horse and wagon together with guides to stalk and obtain trophies for the house and he had been recognised by the guides and other hunters as a good stalker with the calm ability to quietly approach his quarry and use well,directed shots to accomplish his feats.

The Family lived in an imposing two storey house competing with the Manse for pride of place in the building stakes and consisted of Bill, his Mater and Pater, as they liked to be addressed and his eight year old sister Millicent, a shining light in the family and loved to bits by all of them.

That evening Bill sat in the Reading room with his parents 'we are both so proud of you , you can be assured you will be selected' said his Pater 'I have already raised the matter with Captain Smith and providing you pass a medical you are in, and a medical isn't any concern the Doctor will only need one look to see how fit and able you are, so you can look forward to your sojourn with the Army and we know you will serve with honour, do you want a commission when you enlist, I am sure that can be managed as well'

'Thanks for that, the enlistment is only for one year and the war certainly isn't going to be any longer than that, so I would rather just serve with the other chaps until my time is done and I return to home and the farm, if there is another conflict in the future I may well consider a rank but at this time no, I want to share in the camaraderie of the soldiers and try to enjoy the experience unfettered with responsibility'

'So be it, whatever you want, but remember you are not just one of the common mob but our Son and there are privileges which we deserve with our status and these are due to you to as well'

The next morning Bill presented himself at the recruitment office and was advised the medical test has been put off until Friday but everything else is approved at this time ' present yourself on Friday at 9:00 am, you won't have a problem Bill' he was told 'you are just the type the Army needs'

On Friday there was a group of about six others all eager to enlist and awaiting the rigours of a physical examination, to Bills amazement only himself and one other were declared fit to enlist .

What was unknown to him was that the Doctor had been advised that due to the huge number of Volunteers from all over New Zealand for a limited number of positions in the next Contingent that he was only to pass the best standard of NZ youth at this time !

As a result of this instruction the Military Doctor was failing people for Hammer Toes, poor circulation, bad teeth, poor posture and other factors with the advice 'maybe later when we have less stringent entry requirements'

After being passed Bill signed the enlistment papers and made his Oath and was formally inducted into the Army having sworn allegiance to Queen Victoria, the British Empire, New

Zealand etc. alongside the other person accepted who he learnt was a James Merritt from Dunedin.

After the instructions to report for duty the following Monday and other Army information they met on the outside steps 'shake, my name is William, call me Bill, Gibson congratulations it looks like there's only two of us, I hope we can be mates'

'James Merritt, too right, good to meet you, I'm glad that's over and we have been accepted, must have a bit of luck unlike all those others' was the response.

'My train to Taieri doesn't go back until 5:00 this evening and I have a spare afternoon why don't we go and have a drink to celebrate its only 2 o'clock now, my shout' said Bill.

By the end of the afternoon they indeed had begun to form a friendship, they had in common a love of hunting and shooting, a shared liking for horses, had both been in Volunteer forces in the weekends and a joint liking for Speights beer which they were proving by the rate at which they were imbibing, by 4:45 when Bill set off for his train and James set off to trudge home the efficiency and strength of the beer had had an effect on both of them to their detriment but they both agreed it had been a cracker of an afternoon and were already swearing eternal friendship as if they had known one another for years instead of only a few hours.

Needless to state Bill received a pretty cool reception when he got home and the admonishment that 'this is what happens when you associate yourself with a lower type of person I trust this isn't going to continue' from his Pater.

Millicent his golden haired wee sister was however so happy as he told her about his day and how he was now a soldier for the Queen and she would be able to send letters to him while he was away and she at any rate excused his slightly inebriated state as just evidence of how happy he was.

It was a chastened and slower moving Bill that rose the next morning ' well that's that' he thought to himself 'maybe one or two pints too many but what a good time and a new friend'

So began his military journey which he would continue with James at his side as they had hoped.

Chapter 6 : The Combatants –'for New Zealand'

James Merritt and Bill (William) Gibson

'A friendship forged'

On the 26th November James Merritt presented himself at the recruitment office and was advised ' the army requires men of character and strength with good morals, we do not want 'slackers', weaklings or men with other faults and to be honest we have that many volunteers we can 'pick and choose' the best men that New Zealand has, to that end only men who have been in the Volunteer Force or Regulars will be considered, are you one of them ?'

'I consider I am pretty fit and able I am honest and hard working'James said , tongue in cheek,' I am a member of the Otago Volunteer Force and have been for the last year'

Major Smith looked him over , noting the fine physique and stance 'You should stand a good chance, the next assessments and medical are being carried out in 4 days time on Friday starting at 9:00 am , can you be there ?'

James agreed to, and was there, on Friday as instructed with two other young men from the area .

At the end of the morning only two of them, from a total of seven had been accepted into the Army and were to begin training prior to leaving New Zealand ; they were James and Bill Gibson, Bill was a farmers son from Taieri a small settlement about 15 miles South of Dunedin.

They were to sign on for a one year term and would receive four shillings per diem or about one pound ten a week .

'Lets go and have a drink to celebrate' Bill said to James 'my shout, God I am so chuffed that we have been successful'

They struck up an immediate friendship over the afternoon, they were both of a similar build and experienced with the Volunteers, Bill had his own horse, rifle and gear etc. and had been a member of the East Taieri Rifles, they both knew how to shoot and hunt and looked forward to the adventure.

'We will be in our Otago Regiment but I also hope we are in the same squad' said Bill 'I reckon its going to be a great lark, we will see some of the World, be paid for it and have a lot of fun on the way and I am really looking forward to it, I just hope its not over before we get there'

Later that evening it was a cheerful James, albeit a little woozy, that told his Mother and Father and then rushed to Marys to give her the news that he had been accepted and was to begin his training and thence leave for overseas .

The time seemed to fly, except for one weekend off James and Bill were ensconced in camp learning the mysteries of the Military, they were advised that, in spite of requiring to ride horses, for example they would be Infantry not Cavalry, they would be walking and riding, they had to look after their own weapons but would be supplied ammunition and spent considerable time learning marching, the army hierarchy, how to salute, how to clean and polish their equipment, formations for battle, rifle drills and range firing and the blind obedience of orders that is the structure of the forces.

Their final weekend of leave before setting off from New Zealand was a time of reflection and last minute instructions which James spent between his parents and Mary and her Mother and Bill similarly spent with his family, all too soon after tearful farewells, promises to write, tins of baking, photographs and best wishes they were departing Dunedin for Wellington and thence Auckland; Soldiers of the Otago Regiment, No 17 Company, NZ 6th Contingent and who were being sent to replace the 2nd and 3rd Contingents due to be returning home.

As they were assembled and marched to the wharves down Queen Street to the sounds of bands and the cheers of the watchers James chest swelled with pride.' I remember Seddon was determined New Zealand would be the first Colonial force and we were, I just hope I do as well as the others before me have' he thought.

After they had boarded the ship 'S S Cornwall', stowed their gear and horses they were leaning over the ships rail watching the assembled crowds and to the strains of 'God Save our Queen' the vessel began to pull away from the wharf. James turned 'Bill we are finally off , hooray, let the fun begin, I just hope it's not over before we get there there's only a few rebels left for us from the news reports'

06 Feb 1901

Dear Mary

Well we left Auckland on the 30th January and are now well on our way to Australia for our first stop in Albany , hopefully we will get some time ashore .

Bill and I are enjoying the time and the rest of our company which assembled at Auckland before we left .

Just about everyone on board suffered from 'mal de mer' , I think that what its called , anyway we were seasick and stuck it out for a couple of days or so until we got our sea legs

We exercise the horses on deck every day and tend to them , unfortunately , our Vet has ordered one horse 'put down' already as it broke a leg rearing up in the stalls , some of the horses are taking some time getting used to the sea voyage and moving on the deck where we lay out sand every day before exercising them, but they are a good team of steeds and will do us proud.

I will post this letter in Albany when we get there shortly .

Thinking of you with a fond regard , Love

James

20th March 1901

Dear Mater and Pater,

Well here I am in South Africa , well Pretoria actually.

This is a city in the Transvaal and quite an attractive place , it was the base for President Kruger until recently but no one seems to know where he is now.

I fear this is a place of contrasts , its very hot during the day and freezing cold at nights

We were told of two British soldiers out on duty who actually froze to death one night , maybe just a bit of an exaggeration but it sure is cold.

James and I are lucky to be together in A Squadron and we saw a few of our wounded returning a couple of nights ago , they were cheerful and resolute , some even vowing to return after their wounds are attended to. There might be no war left by that time but what an example of the proud New Zealand spirit.

The old hands tell us that the Boer are in almost full retreat now , and only ever attack from cover or lay explosives for trains etc. and we might be lucky to see any action.

I received your fruit cake and the letter from Millicent , both bought me great joy , I can't decide which pleased me the most , at least the fruit cake has double the result as James and I together ate it in one giant sitting.

Must away now , we are to go out on patrol shortly , both of you and Millicent keep well.

Love

Bill

15ᵗʰ March 1901

Dear Mary

Well here we are in South Africa , we disembarked at East London two days ago and after getting sorted and checking our kit and provisions we went by train to Pretoria where I am writing this letter .

This is a big country and the Orange Free State and Transvaal where we are going are apparently about 150,000 square miles which is bigger than New Zealand by about two times I think .

Bill and I are together still in A Squadron under General Plummer and we have about 15 Officers and non coms. from the first three contingents , whom have done their 12 months but signed on again so they are able to tell us about what to expect.

They reckon the war will be over in a few weeks , I do hope we see some action before its all over .

It's a beautiful country and you would like it , warm or hot days but quite cold at nights.

We are to join with Kitcheners force and going to trek towards Pietersburg in North Transvaal later this month and clear the Northern Transvaal of Boers .

I suspect its not going to take long we will be a force of over 8000 and with machine guns and field pieces I suspect the Boers won't know what hit them .

Miss you

Love   James

10ᵗʰ May 1901

Well here I am again , we are now in Pietersburg , we simply walked in without any resistance and this was the Boers temporary capital after Steyn and Kruger (the two ex Presidents) left Pretoria , they must have just about given up all hope now , must surely be nearly over.

We have seen action at Warmbaths and captured some prisoners there and later at Piet Potgeiters Rust (I hope you can find these places on a map)

Bill and I also had a bit of a go with a couple of Boer in the foothills a week ago but the blighters escaped finally .

They took two of our squad with bullets and they were killed and then another was killed when he fell to his death .They were British lads and good fellows but a bit green when it comes to fighting in this type of country.

Makes you think , they were younger than us and so far from their homes as well , mind you that is war.

The Boers are pretty 'sneaky' types with 'hit and run' tactics and won't stop and fight so we chase them all the time although they are hard to catch . They seem to be able to elude us in the scrub and hills – they call them kopjies here , and then they snipe at us from a distance.

They seem pretty good horsemen and are very good shots which isn't so good as they have taken out a few of our troops .

We are just as good but most of the Tommies , while good chaps , are pretty poor horsemen and even worse shots , lucky we have lots of ammunition ha ha .

The Boers we captured are a surly lot , they keep to themselves and sing strange hymns all the time at night , most of them seem lost , they have no uniforms and wear a mixture of rags and animal skins , their shoes or boots are all near worn out and they have a multitude of hats, with the war really lost by now they are in bad shape and obviously just holding on with stubbornness.

We were told they elect their officers from their ranks and if they get sick of them they just vote them out and elect someone else , no wonder they are up against it with our army.

We have been on duty clearing Boer farms to prevent the enemy from reprovisioning and also taking families to camps which we don't like but it seems it is necessary to wear out the Boers resolve to continue.

Apart from that Bill and I are having a good time of it and we are well equipped against the cold nights and is it cold , a couple of the Tommies froze to death one night we are told although not sure if its true .

Anyway , obviously the war can't last much longer , and we will be coming home

I doubt if we will see out our 12 months in Africa

Love

James

6th May near Pietersburg

Dear Mater and Pater

Well some action at last .

We have been with the division and seen action at Warmbaths and Piet Potgeiters Rust a couple of areas here in the North .

We completely outnumbered a force of Commandoes at Warmbaths and after shelling the disused farmhouse where they were holed up we entered the yards to find they had surrendered.

They are a poor looking lot ,moody and depressed , don't say anything and ill kept and dressed in a multitude of different rags , some don't even have proper boots . Lord knows how they have survived so long and they were almost relieved to surrender I think.

We were also on a patrol North with a big force near Piet Potgeiters Rust (where do they get these names) when we saw a couple by themselves and a squad of us where sent in pursuit.

James and I led the way and followed them into a gorge until they set off up a track on the side of the gorge.

Well we were quite a bit in front of the others so dismounted and began firing at them , we think we hit one of them but they scooted to the far side of the track and were hidden from our sight .

A few minutes later the rest of our squad , about ten pulled up and stood by their mounts a bit stupidly in the open and asking 'what did we think' until suddenly one of the Boers must have crawled to the lip of the track and shot one poor chap where he stood and then another as they ran for cover .

We fired back but they had soon disappeared again and we checked the two who had been shot later on but they were both dead.

In spite of the cowardly way in which it was carried out one must have a grudging respect for the marksmanship , its mighty difficult to shoot at a moving target from about 200 yards and hit it as you Pater will know .

37

They also seemed in pretty good shape with good horses so maybe they are new recruits (surely not) , sometime that night they made their escape by following the track up to a plateau and then away to safety .

Goodness me we lost another poor chap as we were following them when he fell over the edge of the track , so one round to the Boer I suppose.

Certainly had our hearts going for a while but exciting at the same time , we are pretty sure we had hit one of them and also one of their horses so with a bit of luck we could have won out.

We are keeping well , everyone keeps saying its soon over and I think they are right , the Boer can't keep this up much longer.

Looking to our return home in the near future.

Love to you both and Millicent

Bill

The Contingent now moved in a sweep through the Middleburg district while the British were driving towards them from the Southwest with the Boers fighting rear guard actions as they retreated, making raids and incursions, mining railway lines and generally proving a nuisance and difficult to find or follow as they utilised their knowledge of the country, its rivers and mountains and how to survive on the minimal rations they had available.

James and Bill had to admire their resourcefulness but still wanted to kill or capture the Boer enemy who by now had been the cause of several of their good mates death and injury .

They have seen action in a variety of environments from open veldts to mountain range, from rivers to dried watercourses and soldiered with the British troops and as smaller ranging units trying to locate and shift the Boers to the waiting Blockhouses and entanglements .

There have been continued successes including Kommander de La Rey defeated on 29th May near Venderstorp with the capture of near 1500 Boers plus considerable field pieces, rifles and ammunition, horses and wagons etc. but still the Boers continue evading in areas and then regrouping to strike again albeit with smaller and smaller resources.

This is now exclusively Guerilla war by the Boers, a strategy which suits the Boers, and is OK by the Colonial troops but is frustrating to the British Army and its, up to now, more structured battles and defensive manoeuvres; in spite of the depleted Boer force more and more troops and resources are being brought to bear but the sheer scale of the country, and some of the terrain, means that men, horses and equipment are feeling the strain.

There have been to date over 450,000 Empire troops and over 200,000 horses with significant losses especially of horses but also men to accidents, wounds, fatalities of battle and disease which has attacked in various guises throughout the years of the war which is now (June 1901) nearing the end of its second year.

Intelligence has reported that the Boers have been receiving shipments of arms from German East Africa via Lourenco Marques, these include rifles, ammunition, Pistols, and light machine guns which have been bought into the Transvaal and are now being hidden in locations near Wonderfontein , it is also reported that Gold reserves have been hidden to make payment for future purchases and that they are being hidden in cemeteries established for war dead .

James and Bill have found themselves in just one of the many cemeteries which have been established near Wonderfontein , albeit, several miles out of the town .

It has many graves, perhaps five hundred, which is disproportional to the population of the area, and contains many victims of the nearby Concentration Camp and war dead.

The Cemetery has been fenced around a perimeter , to protect against ranging animals, one would suspect and has a number of permanent headstones but also a proliferation of graves marked with simple wooden crosses many of which in one area bear several names on each cross.

It is explained these will be deaths from inmates of the Concentration Camps, with a shortage of wood many victims were interned in groups with several children to each makeshift coffin.

'Our intelligence has told us the Boers have hidden arms and ammunition in some of these graves, and others contain Gold reserves to purchase more, your job is to locate and excavate this contraband' the ten squads of six soldiers each are told.

'There are the waiting wagons some of you came on, load anything you find , which will first be recorded by Sergeant Major Ferris so callout if you locate anything; it's not practical or necessary to excavate everything, so only recently dug and filled sites need checking, there seem to be about forty of these so that's about 4 each squad, open any coffins and wear a face mask, your damp handkerchief will d , and rapidly check, avoid breathing the miasma which may contain disease and make sure there doesn't appear to be any additional depth below the coffins, if there is, and the coffins are empty remove them to the side and check below' ' All understood, get to it, its not a pleasant job, the sooner we get it over with , the sooner we all get out of here' admonished the Sergeant .

It was decided that they would take turns with the actual opening of coffins and this was a wise decision, there was limited space in the excavation, but more importantly the first coffin opened by the squad which included James and Bill, had contained six children beginning to decompose and evidently nothing else, the terrible smell and sight caused several of them to turn away and puke beside the grave and it was a rapid backfilling of the grave after that before moving to the next one.

James had been the unlucky first member to undertake the grim task ' All clear' he had called out, slid the coffin lid back and was aided out of the grave before they all rapidly backfilled it and moved to the next recently disturbed site.

As the morning progressed it was apparent the intelligence had been correct, there were cries throughout the morning as Rifles, Ammunition, even a light Machine Gun and other ordinance was located together with several Gold Ingots, perhaps ten in all, from various graves throughout the cemetery.

By early afternoon all of the recently disturbed areas of ground had been addressed, while still not enjoying it the soldiers were becoming inured to the gruesome sites and work, it was of some advantage that when something was located it had been placed atop the corpses and wrapped in oiled cloth so it was pretty simple to pass them out without having to disturb the other contents.

As soon as they reach camp they are stood down to go and get showered and changed and advised ' there is an extra ration of Beer for all at the mess, well done it has been a difficult day but we will have stopped a lot of the Boers resources in this area today' they are told.

James and Bill retire to their tent with the others to remove their clothes to be washed and his mates in the tent are talking among themselves about the day that has just finished 'What a bastard of a job for a man ' one of them comments 'I didn't know I had signed up for this sort of shit, if we had been Boers we would have had a heap of Niggers doing it for us, maybe they weren't so stupid after all' he adds to a general laughter from the others .

'I surely don't intend to tell anyone back home what we have just done, I feel sorry for those kids from the Concentration Camps their Mothers can't be doing much of a job of looking after them, and I am glad we come from a Christian country – be a bloody good thing when it's over and we can get out of here'

'This could be a great country but its wasted on Heathens, I hate the Boers, I hate the heat in the day, I hate the freezing cold nights, I hate the Niggers and I hate waiting to go back home to a civilised country' one of the others added. 'Thank Christ we live in New Zealand she's a corker country all right'

James thinks to himself ' It will do me when I come back with Mary and we set up here, there's a great future after the war and opportunity and we can get some land and be set up for life, its going to change for the better, I can see that' A large number of ex military have already signed up to a new Constabulary to be administered in looking after the country at a rate of pay nearly 4 times the soldiers pay they have been getting for risking their lives.

He has discussed his intentions with Bill and he is supportive of James idea and he had said 'I might stay on for a bit say a few months or so just to see how things pan out, and also I want to do a bit of trophy hunting if I can, but I have the farm and responsibilities back in New Zealand, I can see a great opportunity for you and a wife Mary if she agrees to come, this can be a great place alright once the scrapping is finished'

1st June 1901

Dear Mary

Well here I am again

I have been thinking about our future together.

There is a great opportunity for us in this country , I can get work as a Constable in the new interim Government at a good rate of pay

With careful management and saving I know we could make a go of it here , buy a farm and enjoy a better life

This country has lots of potential and is quite beautiful.

I understand there will be assisted packages for ex servicemen and you and your Mother could come out and have a look at the country and hopefully our future , I have saved a bit myself.

I am sure my best mate Bill would stay on and be our best man before he returns to his family estates (Ha ha wish it was us)

Had a pretty bad time of it lately , we lost three English chaps that were with us and then had some unpleasant work in a cemetery.

The war will soon be over , please consider my suggestion and discuss with your mother , I will tell my folks by separate letter

All my love

James.

3rd June 1901

Wanderfontein

Dear Mater and Pater

Well here I am again still in South Africa.

We have been engaged on a terrible job yesterday disinterring graves where the damned Boers have re opened them and hidden arms and munitions plus gold reserves in some places.

James was the first of us all to take on the terrible task of checking the opened coffins and I must say he has a stronger stomach than I or any of the others although as the day wore on we were slowly getting a little used to it.

Never again I hope what a terrible idea of the Boers , they are little better than animals in some ways .

It only took one day but it was probably the longest day of my life .

Apart from that all is well we are to start driving in great sweeps with thousands of others to drive the Boers towards our barbed wire and blockhouses.

I must confess I am getting a bit sickened of this war it just seems to drag on and on without end and gets worse and worse , the ultimate mans inhumanity on display .

Never mind can't last much longer now and we will soon be home.

Have to be a short letter this time as we are shortly moving out again , thanks for another couple of cakes much appreciated by all.

Love to you both and Millicent

Your loving son Bill

They have missed out on taking place with the great drive where over fifty thousand troops are going to drive the Boers towards the barbed wire entanglements and blockhouses equipped with Maxim machine guns.

In spite of their disappointment and protestations they have been advised they need a bit of an easy job for a while 'The exercise will be a bit of a formality, we will drive the Boers to surrender and it will all be over at last' their Sergeant advises 'I understand although not official that Kitchener is getting a bit of attack at home from the English Press – bastards and he wants mainly British troops in this last decisive offensive – I suppose it won't hurt him to tell everyone us Colonials looked after the camps, so much for appreciating our efforts'

'Bloody British we are going to miss out on all the action to save their faces' was the disgruntled response from Bill endorsed by a violent head shaking by James and the comment 'I will just be glad when it's over , just about had enough anyway'

Their first assignment is to guard the concentration camp boundaries and the inmates, all women and children, watching for any signs of disobedience, on the first day Bill is patrolling the fence near the periphery of the camp above the river bank when he notes a gap in the wire 'Sergeant there is a break in the wire here' he calls out.

'For Christs sake keep your voice down you ignorant Colonial, there is a reason for that and you will find it out one day' was the retort ' now just carry on and keep it to yourself, this is a cushy number don't make work for yourself'

They are living in a tent on the outskirts of the camp with four other New Zealand troops who have all had a varied set of experiences to tell and they begin to swap tales that evening.

'Well we have had experience in digging up graves and opening coffins looking for Boer arms and bullion' said James' and I bet none of you can beat that!'

'We are not even going to try and compete with that, is nothing sacred in this goddam war' one of the others spoke.

'I guess my first thoughts are that this isn't any type of a gentleman's war any more now, I have been at this camp for 3 weeks now and must have seen over fifty children die already, they are going down like flies, poor little buggers, we are told it's because the Boer Mothers don't look after their kids but it's really because they are starving or full of disease from the conditions, they are also on half rations now and I can't see it getting any better, she's a bad thing alright, not what I thought I would be doing when I left New Zealand' one of the others added.

'Yeah and there's a few of the Mothers dying too, you two will see some sights here, some of them look as though they should be dead anyway, so I guess it's not much different to digging up dead ones, just a matter of degree' from a third member of the group.

Bill said 'I got stirred up today when I asked about a hole in the fence down near the far corner alongside the river bank, what was all that about?'

'If you get a bit lonely at night go down there and you will find a few women eager to show you a good time, but take a loaf of bread or some other food they don't need money right now but you will need something to barter with' was the response from one of them

'aren't they worried they might escape' Bill said

'where do you think they would go?, it's about five miles to the mountains and there are still wild animals roaming at night and in the daytime, might just be better in here than attacked by a mob of Hyenas, they get a hard time when they are caught if they try and are locked in the 'box' in the main yard and in this heat I have never seen a live one come back out' ' this is the same army that invented field punishment number one! , the poor buggers are up against it in here it would be bad enough for men but these are women and kids'

For several days Bill and James were occupied walking the perimeter of the camp, checking on people in the tents, after the first two days they have started to come to terms and realize that even if they want too there is nothing they can do for the inmates there is a shortage of food and the soldiers are on basic rations and the internees on half of that.

On day two Bill is standing outside and checking the occupants of tent 107 row 12 and recognises Marie who is sitting near the entrance ' goodness me' he said 'you were on a farm we sacked some weeks ago and had two children with you, how are you all bearing up?' he asked.

'My Daughter died on the train coming here and my son is getting very weak and so am I, can you get us some food please I beg you' Marie cried

'The stupid woman refuses to go to the fence and lift her skirts for a bit of bread, but I don't, want some of what she won't give ?'sneered one of her tent mates Aletta from inside the tent.

'What about both of us for a double bit of bread' called the other Brunelda

Bill turned to Marie 'why don't you take your child to the Doctor?'

'Nobody comes back from the Doctor alive' called out Brunelda from the tent 'anyway there are no medicines as they say they all needed for you troops'

Bill is struck by a memory of his baby sister Millicent back in New Zealand and he is starting to get disillusioned about the conflict, leaning down he whispers to Marie ' meet me at that hole in the fence at 8:00 tonight, don't be afraid'

Marie thinks hard all day 'can I trust a soldier , what if he attacks or rapes me or says I am trying to escape, I must decide and I have to do something to possibly save Johannes and this may be my only chance' she leaves the tent just before 8:00 that night and asks Aletta 'will you please watch Johannes for me I shan't be long'

'Yes I aren't going out tonight, good luck, thought you would see the light before long , enjoy yourself and don't do anything I wouldn't do' she laughs.

Marie reaches the fence at 8:00 and is accosted by a couple of English soldiers ' what are you offering missus' they say 'come with us and see what we have got!'

'Leave her alone you two' is the message as Bill arrives 'she wants to see me'

'Keep your hair on mate, there's no shortage you can have her, a bit old for us anyway'

'Come with me' says Bill grasping her hand and pulling her towards the river bank where numerous other couples are engaged in all sorts of activities accompanied by groans, cries and moaning ' we have to stay here and be still for a while at least then you can go' he adds 'I have brought a slice of bread it's all I could salvage from my meal but hopefully it will give you a little more food and I can get some more again tomorrow or the day after'

'why are you doing this' Marie asks 'you owe me nothing, you were one of them that destroyed our farm and no one else helps us'

'I wonder if anyone would help my little sister if anything untoward happened, I am a New Zealander and we don't usually treat people like you are being treated, I don't know why I picked you, I recalled you from the farm and was just struck by how forlorn you looked and decided I could do some small thing for someone, I have no other motives'

They lay on the bank side by side 'what is New Zealand like?' asks Marie

'it's a great country with lots of green forests, beaches are nice and the mountains are very scenic a little bit like parts of your country, my family owns a big holding and we are quite well off, the nights are clear just like here and the same constellations in the sky, that's the Southern Cross or the Pleiades set of stars' he pointed out 'funny that it's just the same here, although its shape has rotated around a bit, as it is half a world away from my home'

'we call that the 'kite' responded Marie and 'our people used it for navigation during the great trek but also to find our way around sometimes'

Later that night Bill returned to his tent 'where have you been?' asked James 'not to the hole in the fence I hope'

'actually I have' answered Bill and proceeded to tell James what he had done.

'well mate you are a better man than me, good on you for trying to help someone but I suspect it's a lost cause' James responded ' this place is just full of the poor damned, right now I almost hate the British as much as the Boers, they are both animals'

Back at Marie's tent both Aletta and Brunelda were pestering Marie, ' how did it go , what did you get up to ?' they questioned but Marie was reticent and determined not to discuss what had transpired while she shared her small repast with Johannes.

A short time later and Johannes was violently ill in the tent, shaking uncontrollably and with a fevered brow 'well that was a waste of food' sneered Aletta 'it looks like he has either Malaria or some other disease which are rampant around here'.

Marie was beside herself as she thought 'finally something was coming right and now this the same day' she picked up Johannes and ran towards the Hospital and burst into the hospital tent ' please do something for my son' she cried.

A nurse attended and looked him over and took his temperature and checked his eyes and breathing and turned to Marie 'I am so sorry, your child appears to have Malaria, we have no quinine as its all required for our troops and you must prepare yourself as it is unlikely he will survive the night, you must leave him here tonight and return in the morning'

'Can't I stay with him' Marie pleads.

We certainly don't have any spare room away with you and come back in the morning" is the response.

With a leaden heart Marie trudged back to the tent 'we are so sorry' both Aletta and Brunelda said 'we know we have been a bit cruel in the past, but it's such a shame about Johannes he is a brave wee lad and maybe things will be alright, we really do hope so for your sake'

Marie sobbed into her pillow that night and in the morning rushed to the hospital and was met by the same Nurse 'your poor child passed away last night, he did not suffer, would you like to say goodbye'.

Marie sobbed over the prone body lying at peace with several others as a Sergeant and several soldiers appeared 'you must finish your goodbyes, you have ten minutes with your deceased and they will then be removed for internment, we do not have enough wood for coffins and your children will be buried with others in canvas shrouds, you may not attend the service but I can assure you that our Padre will perform a Christian service for your children and their graves will be marked'

September 1901

My Dearest Wilhelm

I do not know if you will ever receive this letter but I am told somehow it will be delivered to you , one of the soldiers has said they will somehow get it to one of your groups and I must trust him.

I remember so well our first times when we met and you courted me under the watchful eyes of my parents and the happy days we had on our little farm raising our two children and our life together

How I shall miss you

Our dear wee girl Mariette died on the train taking us to this terrible camp and today our son Johannes has passed to the lord also and I am bereft.

I loved you so much but I cannot go on now all alone

I trust you keep well and survive to make a new life for yourself

I just cannot believe we are ever going to win this war and our country may never recover

Goodbye my love

Marie

It is two days later and Bill returns to tent 107 row 12 and calls out to the occupants 'hello is Marie there can I talk to her'

A saddened Brunelda says 'Marie is dead, her child died two days ago, and she hung herself from the centre pole of our tent while Aletta and I were out at the fence last night, she must have used the bucket to stand on the poor woman, she was devastated after Johannes died and we didn't realize she had taken it to heart so, what a terrible end for her, may she find some peace with God from this awful place, there nothing for you now so piss off and leave us to mourn her'

A chastened Bill slowly walks away from the tent thinking 'I haven't done anything to help that poor woman, I foolishly thought I could make some small difference in this place but I guess we are all powerless at the end of the day what a tragedy'

That night he speaks to James 'I guess we all do some things in life we regret and one of them was coming here, it's a great country but it's a terrible place in the middle of this stinking war, I wish the Boer would chuck it in and we could go and have a bit of a look around after the war while you wait for your Mary and her Mother, heard any more and am I going to be needed as a best man?'

'I haven't had an answer back yet, but you will be the first to know, I know how you feel about the war, certainly wasn't the adventure I was looking for and like you the sooner it's over the better'

The war continued to be waged in a series of guerrilla attacks by the Boers and response from the Empire forces with little effect and it dragged on from the end of 1901 into 1902.

The significant success of the Empire forces has been the routing of the Boer forces under de la Rey defeated near Ventersdorp in June 1901.

Bill and James had continued in their Concentration Camp policing role and grew more and more disillusioned each day as the struggle dragged on.

The Empire forces were massing near their western front which extended from just east of Johannesburg and Pretoria north to the edges of occupied Transvaal and were to begin a push towards the East to entrap the Boers against the border of Swaziland where the British Blockhouses and machine guns would ensure a decisive blow to the Boers and an expected surrender.

To James and Bills delight they were again to see action as part of the fifty thousand troops as they prepared to join the offensive above and they were looking forward to the end of the war at last.

October 1901

Dunedin

Dear James

If you think we can be happy in South Africa after the war , then yes I will come out for our wedding after the war is over

Mother will not come to live but will come with me as a chaperone and to attend on the wedding.

I do hope you have thought carefully it s a big move but I know how you struggled to find a permanent job before you left and if our opportunity is to be there , so be it

I am so happy with the ring you have sent to bind us in an engagement

Mother and I so look forward to seeing you shortly , the papers here all speak of the major offensive and that the end is imminent and a jolly good show I say.

We are all well here , I have told all my friends and they are so happy for us

Love

Mary

Dunedin

October 1901

Dearest James

What a shock to receive your letter

Are you sure you want to go ahead with taking Mary to a foreign country to be married there away from all her friends and family.

Your Father is so angry he refuses to discuss it with me and I am not sure if we could afford to come out to South Africa for your wedding , he won't tell me the state of our finances and whether or not we could afford it.

What on earth does Mary and her Mother think of your idea, oh dear I suppose if there are to be better opportunities to make something of your life then I must be happy for you.

Your Brother sends his best wishes and seems to agree it can be a great country with lots of natural wealth and good land and says he supports you if that's what you want to do

I love you very much and it will sadden me if you do not return and I am unable to see you again

On a happier note it seems that the war will be over shortly and that is really good news , I have been so worried for your safety on the battlefield

All a Mothers love and I am sure your Fathers regards

Mother

It is February 1902 and James and Bill have joined almost forty five thousand troops and field pieces plus hundreds of wagons, horses and oxen to begin the great drive towards the Swaziland border instillations

De Wet of the Boer forces has however taken his Kommando South towards the Cape Colony and General French has decided that two of the columns will pursue him and this has left a gap on the Northern side of the line, however, able to be covered by the column of Colonel Campbell (admittedly a bit smaller than the other eight columns as a result of some of his command joining the two columns in pursuit of De Wet).

It is also considered unlikely Boers will attempt escape by this avenue anyway but that is exactly what is going to happen and in fact most of the Boers including the Kommandos of Beyers and Louis Botha have eluded the British and are now roving free behind the great front.

At this time James and Bill along with everyone else do not know what is to transpire and are jubilant that they are going to see some action again

'It is great to back on a horse and heading towards what must be a final front and some action again' says Bill' I have been stagnating in that bloody concentration camp, after that poor woman and her son died almost together and to see the same thing going on day after day has just worn me down, how the human race, us included can be so barbaric amazes me'

After two weeks they are beginning to near the Swaziland border without firing a shot.

'we must be nearly upon them or else they are going to run into our Blockhouses and machine guns' says James 'where are they all anyway, there certainly is no shortage of us'

The next day they begin to hear the sounds of battle in the distance ' alright all saddle up, we are about to engage the enemy' calls their Sergeant 'form up by the right and slow canter boys let's put an end to this lot'

Soon they near a group of about two hundred Boer soldiers assembled and holding erect a white flag, together with their mounts wagons and oxen plus a couple of field guns they look in pretty poor condition, in a multitude of motley dirty dusty clothes they present a sorry sight.

Together with a Colonel commanding perhaps another five hundred troops they encircle the Boer and they lay down their arms.

'not really a lot of action was it' says Bill to James and their platoon of soldiers 'I wonder what the firing was'

That night the assembled Army has altogether taken nearly two thousand Boer captive, there has been minimal firing or engagement with the Boer obviously realizing they were trapped between the advancing forces from behind and being directed towards certain disaster at the Machine guns lined out in front of them. They are temporarily guarded, after having been fed and watered and some of them have indicated this has been the first food they have had for several days.

That appears to be the limit of the success of the operation however, somehow the bulk of the Boer main force has eluded the Empire forces and seems to have escaped in a number of directions and are taking refuge in the mountainous areas or making their way to link up with De Wet and his significant force now nearly at the Cape Colony border to the South.

For the next week they were engaged in constructing a camp for the captured Boers arranging fencing and constructing blockhouses at the corners of the camp, erecting tents and constructing latrines all the time provisioning themselves and the Boers who now they have surrendered seem pretty reconciled to their fate and reasonably happy that at least their war is over.

At nights they can be heard singing their dirge like Hymns and talking either to each other or some of the guards who they constantly mock asking if they are worried that they haven't got enough troops to take the Boer forces?

Some of the reactions to these taunts are quite heated especially when the Boer remind them that the Empire forces have had about five thousand manning the Blockhouses and barbed wire fences with another fifty thousand or so to pursue them for over two months for a measly two thousand prisoners, a ratio of about thirty to one!

'Well James, here we are guarding another concentration camp, at least this one isn't full of women and children' Bill said ' maybe this is to be the story of our war until the end whenever that is going to be, I thought the British Generals and Kitchener had decided this was going to be the decisive battle and end the war, so much for that idea' he scoffs ' there was hardly any fighting anyway, look at the poor buggers they are finished but just won't lie down and quit'

The Colonial troops and a number of others are ensconced near the prisoners camp and are established in their own tents and facilities and are only sending out small patrols and maintaining sentry duties against a few marauding Boers that have sought shelter and refuge in the high ridge and range near Wolverfontein constantly moving about while British field guns pound the hills every time they spot a bit of movement, the commanders are reluctant to engage them in this type of country knowing the accuracy of their sniper fire and ability to disappear as soon as they are threatened, at least there is only a few small Kommandos and they are almost regarded more as a nuisance than a threat and are contained by the field guns and patrols anyway.

Bankfontein about 12 miles south of Middleburg

Saturday 15th February 1902

My dear Mary

I have had to give you directions above so you can find us on a map.

We have been with the great Eastern Trek to end the war unfortunately the Boer didn't see it that way and although we have captured about 2 thousand of them most have escaped again and are all over the place.

Its getting pretty cold here at nights with Winter only a couple of months away and we sit talking around a brazier most night with a cup or so of Tea to enjoy the company and the chat.

The English are good blokes and enjoy a bit of a laugh but are a bit out of their league (actually completely out of their league) fighting these Boers when they are behind cover as they are very good shots and the Boer snipers shake them up a bit !!

Well we are now guarding about 2 thousand Boer prisoners and its pretty boring work I don't think they are at all interested in escaping in fact one of them told me in their mixed up English etc that he was enjoying the food and not having to worry about being blown up by one of our shells.

Its great news that both you and your Mother will be coming over , your Mother at least until our wedding

Well can't be long now , I keep saying that sooner or later it must be true. How they hold on I don't know there can't even be many left. Stubborn blighters!!

Hopefully will be together soon

All my love

James

Near Middleburg

20th April 1902

Dear Mater and Pater

I trust this finds you both well as am I

James and I are still together and have been alternately guarding the Boer prisoners or out on roving patrols

There are still pockets of Boers in the hills and mountains and they still foray out to the front do a bit of sniping then retreat to the cover of the hills again

The British troops seem pretty ineffectual in this environment but we and the Aussies seem to be a bit better and more successful in that environment so we get a bit more action.

There is also a rough rider sort of a group of Aussies formed from ex Gold Miners that were here before the war and they seem pretty ruthless and also successful

They have Aboriginal trackers with them and I have heard from some of the Boers we capture when they surrender they are a bit afraid of them and their policy of 'take no prisoners'

Such is war there doesn't seem to be anything gentlemanly about any of it now and I wish it was over!

Apparently Louis Botha elected by the Boers to negotiate went to see Kitchener at Middleburg to sue for peace before Winter but they wouldn't agree to Kitcheners terms so here we are still.

I certainly don't intend to sign on for another year if its still going after Winter when my second year will be over but I will stay around and have a good look . James is of a similar mind and maybe we wait until his fiancée and her Mother turn up I can do my duty as Best Man and then think about coming home , plenty of work available here now for James as large parts of South Africa are now free of the war and returning to normal

Give my love to Millicent she will have been growing up while I am away and I am so looking forward to seeing you all again.

Love to you both

William (Bill)

James and Bill have continued a policy of scouting and had several small skirmishes but the war finally seems to be slowing to a halt and the onset of winter is not a prospect to look forward too.

31st May 1902 is an auspicious date, finally the war is ended with the treaty signed at Vereeniging ending hostilities, the Treaty recognizes a British Military administration of both the Orange Free State and Transvaal.

There is great celebration in the camp that night with an extra ration of cigarettes and beer for all the troops who gather until late that night exchanging stories, tales of loved ones and what their intentions are after the war.

2nd May 1902

Dearest Mary

Its over finally the Boer have surrendered

We just have a bit of mopping up to do , the British troops are going home before most of us Colonial forces .

The tent camps are in the process of being collapsed and packed for transit back to England

Tomorrow we set off on patrols to find the last lots of Boer fighters and bring them news of the surrender and to bring them to camp to be signed of and sent back home , whatever that is, I fear there isn't much left for many of them.

We can sign off shortly and stay if we want to , I am of course and Bill has decided he is going to go hunting while he stays on until our wedding

Great news and looking forward to you and your Mother being able to begin making arrangements to come over

In the meantime I am going to sign up to the constabulary role and accumulate some funds and look at what land we can acquire

My deepest love

James

2nd May 1902

Dear Mater , Pater and Millicent

Well at last it is over

I know I have been saying it for a while but this time its true

We have some duties yet but are able to sign off shortly and stay if we want and that is what I am going to do. I will send you a bank to transfer funds to and perhaps you can see your way to lodging some funds, say one hundred pounds for me, (see below)

I am going to stay on for at least a couple of months, dependent on how James' arrangements for his wedding go, for in any event we are unlikely to be able to return until the British soldiers have been sent home which at this rate is going to be a couple of months anyway.

I am going to engage in some guided hunting trips , there are some magnificent game animals here and we can adorn the walls of the estates when I finally get home and have some trophies sent out

It has been an experience I don't / wouldn't want to repeat and it will be great to finally get back to good old New Zealand (It really is Gods own country)

I have a few souvenirs which I will sent in advance and keep in touch

Your loving son and brother

Bill (William)

The next day they are despatched with a group of others to seek out Boer groups and bring them back to camp, to record their details and complete the paperwork required by the Military before they are to be sent back to their farms.

Readers Note: In fact it is not possible for the great bulk of farmers (for that is all the Boers ever were !) to return to their farms with poisoned crops , stock all taken or dead and no buildings left and many will join their families and live in the tents and facilities of the concentration camps while the authorities try and put some semblance of order back into the country before they can resume a normal life. The British Government will pay millions in reparations to re establish the farms or new alternatives and within a short time will again then cede the country back to the Boers !

Chapter 7 : The Combatants – 'for South Africa'

Louis Badenhorst

1885 Transvaal to March 1901

Louis was a big lad of strong build and defined features, he carried an arrogance not befitting one of his age and treated his Fathers slaves with a contempt and scorn although he was only 9 years old in 1885. He did have a few friends among the boy slaves on the farm that he played with pretending hunting, kicking balls made from animal skins around and generally exploring but there was always a reticence to get to close and they always knew he was to be the leader in everything they did.

He had been introduced to the Mauser rifles they had on the farm and been trained in their use from about 8 years old until his shoulders ached from the recoil of the 8mm x57mm ammunition and he began to flinch as he pulled the trigger, his Father would beat him about the head berating him to 'hold it in to your shoulder tight and stand like a man' he would rant until slowly he began to come to terms with it and achieve some success 'you have to learn to survive out here boy and you had better do it fast if you intend to survive' he was exhorted.

His Father was a big man with a brusque manner, never once in Louis' memory had he ever told him he had done something right and his life was filled with criticism and almost daily wallops around his head and body.

His Mother had died in childbirth and his Father had never remarried seeking solace in the bottles of native beer and on occasions a better class of brewed product, when he ever had occasion to travel to Pretoria or other towns, and companionship with whichever of the towns or farms black girls took his fancy from time to time.

The farm was ruled with an iron fist and woe betide any of the slaves who were ruled to have misbehaved and Louis as well.

There were about 20 African children on the farm as slaves, the Boers had earlier decided that keeping 'inboekselings' could help in by teaching them the life and customs of Boers so that they would be assimilated into the society, learn the word of God and spread the word among their tribes when they were 'set free' generally in their early twenties. This may have been at least partly successful in many environments but the stark reality of the Badenhorst farm was that to the contrary it was extremely likely that most would leave with an ingrained hatred of the farmers in general and Louis' Father in particular.

From time to time his neighbours would call and discuss the weather, the animals and crops and general matters of state . They would often be accompanied by their wives and children with the women attempting to promote their Daughters abilities and fine upbringing for his Father would have been a good catch for a young lady with his property and assets, this latter to no avail as he had no interest in remarrying whatsoever.

There were four families in the area, their closest neighbour was Wilhelm de Bruin Senior with his son of the same name and about the same age as Louis so they enjoyed the occasions when they were able to meet and play together.

The families usually stayed overnight, at least and often longer, due to the distance between farms and the slow travel especially if they were travelling by oxen pulled wagons to trade.

At night after supper the men, for there were sometimes more than one neighbour calling, would sit around the fire at night puffing on their cob pipes and talking and Louis and his childhood friends would sit quietly and they hoped unobtrusively while they listened to the talks of their parents.

They were usually reminiscences of the great Trek, the search for new land and an independent state beyond the British influence to the North. About 12,000 Boers had progressively over the period 1835 for the next decade left the security of the South and trekked North in many parties and with various leaders but with a common goal.

The Boer (Boere) were pastoral farmers, in fact the word Boer means farmer and they were all Dutch speaking and their language became Afrikaans with a mixture of Dutch , French, Malay, German and Black influences and their own type of Calvinist religion they had been forced to adapt as none of their own church leaders or synods would endorse or go with the Trekkers.

They had travelled in 'Jawbone' wagons so called because of their shape and had been very light so as not to strain the oxen and able to negotiate the veldt, narrow ravines, rivers and steep escarpments they encountered on their journey. They battled hea , cold, and had to adapt for example when they encountered the Drackensburg slope 3500 metres long where no wagon brakes or oxen could slow the descent of a wagon and instead they had removed the rear wheels and tied large logs beneath the wagons to slow the speed to a controlled pace.

They had avoided the Tsetse fly belt and the Kalahari desert and finally found central highlands each side of the Vaal River where they had settled and finally been recognised as independent states by Britain at the 'Sand River' talks in 1852 .

The children were entranced by the tales of hardship and sacrifice and took a great pride in their heritage.

They were regaled with tales of the battles against the occupying natives who had resisted what they had seen as an invasion and how the wagons had been formed into a circle with the wheels filled with branches to make a barrier and allow firing slots and a place to hide. The women and children were tasked with reloading the multiple muzzle loaders each Trekker carried and Louis' Father had been with Potgeiter when 40 Boers had beaten off a force of 6000 Ndebele warriors, leaving 430 killed with no Boer fatalities although thousands of sheep, oxen and cattle had been lost and his Father seemed to embellish the tale until it became more and more exaggerated with each telling .

The men each told stories of strength and fortitude and then would close with singing a few of their hymns, the less told about these the better as most were an almost continuous dirge and were generally pretty lacking in enjoyment for the children.

On this day Louis and his Father accompanied by four of the older 'boys' were hunting the veldt for Springbok, these were a valuable resource being a source of meat and hides plus other pieces for example the skin for sausages from the intestines and sinews for strong bindings etc.

Springbok were only found on the treeless veldt which offered them some security from Leopards although they were still prey for many other species including Jackals, wild dogs and humans and thus were constantly alert and observant.

It was now mid afternoon and Louis and one of the 'boys' had been crawling on their bellies for nearly two hundred metres now towards the herd of Springbok and Louis decided this was close enough, he lifted up slightly and took up his position and aimed his Fathers Mauser rifle at what appeared to be the biggest animal took a deep breath and squeezed the trigger as he had been taught.

He must have flinched involuntary as the shot went off, the animal lurched but to his amazement did not fall and began to stagger off, the balance of the herd had bolted, leaping into the air with a series of great jumps which rapidly took them into the distance. Louis rose up and watched the animal he had shot at moving away attempting to keep the erratic gait of its species but in obvious distress.

'You stupid fool, I have taught you how to shoot properly and you have only wounded the poor bloody thing' roared his father while cuffing him roundly about his head ' why didn't you put another shot into it while you could, now its out of range' he added ' the bullet was bloody near as big as the poor little thing and you had better go and get it'

'You can take two of the boys, I am going back to the farm and you had better return with that animal when you have finished it off and no excuses find your way home' he threw a packet of Bells wax vestas matches towards him 'take these, if you have to stay out tonight you had better light a fire lest the Lions or Hyenas get you and you might need to stay warm'

Louis was about to protest until he glanced at his Fathers visage which was red and he could sense his apoplectic rage boiling there and decided he had better get moving and he set off after the animal with two of the wide eyed 'boys' who weren't looking forward to this any more than Louis !

As they trudged after the wounded animal Louis looked back and saw his Father storming off in the direction of the farm and realized he truly was alone with the two 'boys'; it was easy to follow the trail as the Bok had not been able to take the giant leaps of its type and occasionally there were small drops of blood and it was obvious the shot had not struck a vital spot but probably 'gut' shot the poor thing and it must have been in agony.

It was evening when they caught up to the Springbok, it stood sides heaving and seemingly unable to move as they approached until Louis felled it this time with a clean shot.

The three of them rushed forward and he rapidly began to sever the head and gut and clean the carcase and they loaded it onto one of the 'boys' to carry over his shoulders Louis guessed it weighed about 25 kg which was about the average size for Springbok and if they took turns they should be able to make the farm that night and accordingly they set off at a good pace.

They soon slowed down the 'boys' were only about 13 or 14 years old and the weight began to be telling for them Louis was really struggling when he tried to take a turn and the other two told him not to bother trying but to watch out for Lions and other unfriendly animals on their journey.

Soon it began to get dark, Louis could see the Southern Cross in the sky so knew which way was home but the temperature was beginning to drop and they were getting cold, soon he instructed the carrier to take a rest while he and the other began urgently seeking out clumps of grasses and dung to make a fire, that night they huddled together around the fire while beyond the extent of their vision they could hear large animals circling and see sometimes the reflection of the fire in their eyes. Louis kept the rifle loaded by his side and the three of them were united in their joint terror of the night and fearful of the animals but huddled together talking to one another to keep awake and from time to time began to chant songs to keep their spirits up.

Finally came the dawn and the realization that there were three Lions, a mother and two cubs and beyond them several Hyenas circling their small encampment.

It was obvious they would be in extreme danger if they had to carry the carcase while trying to protect their rear from attack and they urged Louis to shoot the female Lion so that they could make their escape.

The Lioness was perhaps only about 50 metres away as Louis lay resting the rifle on the back of one of the prone bodies of the boys and he carefully lined up the giant head remembering his Fathers instruction when shooting cattle 'X marks the spot and aim for the cross between the ears and the eyes', this time he squeezed off the shot making certain he did not flinch and the shot was true and the Lioness collapsed dead to the ground.

'You are a great hunter' the boys chanted while dancing about in glee 'you have saved us all' and indeed Louis felt a pride in himself at what had actually been a pretty simple shot 'take the skin, take the skin' they added and so they began the task of skinning out the large beast while the now orphan cubs cowered close to the body.

As they walked towards the farm they were a happy crew now, behind them the Hyenas had killed the Lion cubs and were attacking the carcase of the Lioness with no interest in the trio.

Later that day they neared the farm and the 'boys' began to call out 'we are home with the great hunter' as the farm buildings and workers came into view.

Louis was so proud as they deposited the Springbok to be hung and butchered and the Lioness skin to be tanned

' Lucky for you' snorted his Father 'you are back and all alive, must have done something right for a change' and he turned back to his work.

At that moment a deep hate began to form in Louis' 'one day I will give you some of your own back you miserable bastard' he thought.

Over the next several years he continues his work while still being berated by his Father but his continuing improvements in hunting for the farm and his way with the 'boys' plus his growing stature and size mean that his life is slowly improving and he has become a fine shot and able to look after himself in any circumstance often staying out overnight with one or more of the 'boys' on hunting and exploring trips on foot but more usually on horseback with the natives jogging alongside.

Finally one day when he is sixteen his Father again strikes out at him for some slight, Louis rises to his feet 'that's the last time you will do that' he yells as he throws a punch which misses 'you young ingrate you won't do that again' sneers his Father as he deals a telling blow to his stomach which doubles him up with pain and he slumps to the ground where his Father delivers a kick to his head and begins to walk away.

Louis rises to his feet and rushes towards his Fathers back and delivers a kidney punch and he watches as he collapses to the ground 'you will regret that' he calls as he falls.

Louis realizes this is the moment he must stand or fall right now and as his Father rises he delivers a couple of punches to his head and watches as he spits out one of his teeth. When next he attempts to rise Louis kicks him back to the ground and begins to kick him in the stomach and side as he writhes on the ground cursing and swearing all the time and threatening revenge when he gets up.

Louis continues the assault until finally his Father lies prone on the ground and near unconscious until Louis throws a bucket of water over him 'have you had enough or do I carry on for I will kill you if I have to'

'I think you have broken my ribs and damaged my insides' is the response 'don't do any more I need attention'

Louis instructs a couple of the 'boys and girls' to attend on him as he walks away, the start of a new environment on the farm and a new life for him. His Father slowly recovers over several weeks but is a chastened man and he morosely walks the farm after that murmuring to himself and taking out his anger on the farm workers.

Years later and Louis is now 25 years old and effectively managing the farm. He is aware of the war that had started in 1899 and of the gradual defeat of the Boers and their retrenchment and development of guerrilla warfare harassing the Empire forces and begins to think that maybe he should contribute to the effort, The Orange Free State has been annexed and it looks like Transvaal is not far from a similar fate but like many others he feels the Empire forces won't have the stomach for a protracted guerrilla war and will soon tire and leave them in peace.

One morning a soldier rides onto the farm and delivers a note calling on them to sign a form of allegiance or suffer the consequences, Louis is outraged and storms about the farm until his neighbour Wilhelm de Bruin rides up and says he is going to meet their other neighbours and have a meeting to see what they are to do about it

'I already know but I will see you in two days' says Louis.

Chapter 8 : The Combatants – for South Africa

Wilhelm and Louis - Transvaal

March 1901

Wilhelm de Bruin sat at the table in his cob farmhouse planted in the South African Veldt, Transvaal, three of his neighbours had ridden several miles each to join him and discuss what they were to do with the notices that had recently been delivered to each of them.

A Khaki Corporal had ridden his bicycle to each of their farms and delivered a form to each of the Boers (farmers), they read .

'Be advised you are required to sign an 'Oath of Allegiance to Queen Victoria and the Empire' by you solemn Oath and that you will not aid or abet the Rebel Republicans in this war against the Sovereignty of the Queen.– stating you will not give support to the Republican Rebels who continue a state of war against the Empire.

With such an oath and allegiance you may continue to farm your lands free of any further requirements.

signed   Lieut,General Sir J. French

They had sat drinking Wilhelms beer, smoking their pipes, discussing the weather and their families and contemplating what to do next.

Wilhelm de Bruin was a big raw boned man with a generous beard which could'nt hide the smile which usually was on his countenance, he was not smiling today though, in fact , he appeared like a wild man .

'By God these British have a damned cheek, how much more from us do they want, why should we sign their bloody form'

'There are now more than 350,000 of them , and growing every day, and we only have the bare bones of our rebel forces left, I understand from my visit to Klerksdorp last month we have less than 20,000 left fighting for freedom anyway, I kept out of it when we mobilised before but I am of a mind to join the rebels, their guerrilla tactics seem to be working, the bloody Brits have no answer and are pretty poor troops anyway, I say lets go to their aid until they decide to leave us alone again and restore the independence that we had before the war'

'I am with you' said Louis Badenhorst , his closest neighbour, Louis was also big, but boisterous and bronzed with a clean face, roughly shaved and burnt with a candle to trim, with a well known fiery temper, men knew to hold their piece until he had spoken .

'They must be getting sick of the fighting, the Colonials are a bit of a handful but the Brits will send them home soon if we set up a bit of resistance and then they will clear off themselves . They have burnt up a few farms and taken a few families of our troops and their slaves to the concentration camps but they are going to get tired of fighting and having to keep them all.'

'If we can stick it out, God willing we will win a war of attrition, we can keep up our 'hit and run' for ever if we have to, the Brits are'nt going to stick it out much longer, they have had a year already, I am told in spite of not liking our policy of having slaves they are going to start the Blacks working in the mines in Transvaal, we can let them have that a bit of a concession if we have to and that might move them along'

'They just need a few more losses and I reckon they will be open to a bit of bargaining, stay firm and we will get our Free State back!'

'There's a limit to how many more families they could stick in their camps, they are full now both with burgher families and the others with slaves, hold resolute, I say fight'

'*The Lord will be with us , trust in him with all your hearts and lean not on your own understanding*' 'Our cause is just and he won't forsake us' he quoted from Proverbs.

The other neighbours had sat silently till now, both Andries Bakkes and Paul Steytler were of same mould as Wilhelm and Louis, big, gruff, resolute men but Louis stared with ill disguised contempt as Andreis spoke.

'It's a bloody lost cause, I reckon there will be more troops coming yet for the Brits, our commanders have ceded Orange Free State and Transvaal and Oom Kruger is in Europe now so we don't have a President. Let's just try and make things normal again. We just have to sign the oath and its finished ; I for one have no intention of joining the rebels in a lost cause and you two should reconsider to , what about your families ?'

'For Christs sake man, they can't get any more troops than they have now, they must be thinking of downsizing their force and thinking about leaving, stick it out and we will win victory' was Wilhelm's response 'we have to be united and make the sacrifice or we can't hold our heads high ever again.'

'If you have decided to give up and cede everything, what possessed you to come here tonight, its sounds like you have already made up your minds, are you going to join the other handsoppers (hands uppers) who have already given up their freedom – join us , be men , and fight for whats ours, we already rejected the British way of life, our fathers travelled the 'great trek' for us and Britain recognised our Transvaal and Orange Free State at Blonfontain in 1854, stand up and be counted'

Paul drew himself up ' don't speak for us man , we came here because we thought you two might be headstrong enough to join the rebels, we wanted to try to convince you to side with us, sign the Oath, and lets get the fighting over so that we, and our families, can enjoy some peace at last. We are sick of the conflict, we don't agree the Brits are likely to give up now and every day more troops arrive , it's a lost cause, we can rebuild if we can stop the fighting'

'Piss off if you are not with us, we will do what has to be done ourselves' Louis roared 'go on get away out of my sight or you will regret it'

Wilhelm could feel the situation was getting out of control 'let's just all calm down, if you aren't coming so be it but you are not going to convince me not to join and fight with our countrymen'

'I am sorry it has come to this' Paul said 'we are completely at odds with each other , you and Louis, Wilhelm do what you must, we will look after your families in your absence, until you return and now there is nothing more to say' and he extended his hand.

Readers Note: The circumstance changed rapidly and within weeks the formalities were over and all Boer farms were destroyed and the occupants committed to the concentration camps irrespective of any allegiance or otherwise!

Wilhelm reached forward and took his hand and turned to Andries to shake his hand.

'I will not shake the hand of a coward and a traitor to our cause, I told you before to 'piss off' and I suggest you do so right now' Louis stood and glared .

As they walked off to their mounts to return home Paul said ' we will still look after your women and childre , good luck to you, you will need it'

Wilhelm said 'I have prepared for this day, I have my Mauser and 30 rounds of ammunition and food for 8 eight days, I have to say goodbye to Marie and the children and I am ready to go, we are to meet the Kommando near Rhenestor Kop and assemble there, how long will it take you to ready Louis ? '

'We will go tomorrow morning, call at my farm on your way out and we are off!' Louis responded . 'there's no time to waste , let's get going and do it'

That night Wilhelm and Marie had spent the night in each others arms after making love thinking all the time of his farewell and whispered to each other through the night ' I am certain you and the children will be alright' Wilhelm said 'the British are a civilised people and the tales of the camps must be exaggerated, it won't be long I am sure and we will be reunited, I have to go and try to save our country, if I fail so be it the Lord will decide'

It was a worried Wilhelm that bid his wife Marie and their two children Johannes and Marriette goodbye 'you are the man of the family' he told Johannes, his eight year old son and to Marriette aged six 'help your Mother while I am gone, it won't be long and you will all be alright, keep the stock fed, tend to the crops and stay cheerful for me till I return'

His mount was laden with his sleeping gear, bedroll, rifle scabbard and food and drink prepared the night before by Marie.

'You may leave , if you want' he told Mollie and Mason the Black house servants.

Mollie had cleaned the house and gardens through the years, but more importantly had assisted in raising the children and Mason had been the farm hand and general worker. They were both in their sixties and had known no other life.

Wilhelms Father had bought them as children when the property ran more slaves and they were the last left. For the last 40 years they had lived as man and wife in their branch and daub hut with a thatch roof and bare floor 'we will stay and help the Mama and children' replied Mason 'good luck to you Master we look to your return'

Wilhelm swung to his horse, 'goodbye' he called with a wave as he rode North to meet Louis

They had about 4 days of hard riding in front of them, that was providing they did'nt meet up with any of the roving patrols on route, so they spurred their horses and rode off.

'We have to head about due North so we can use the Southern Cross at night to maintain our direction, simply keep it directly behind our backs' Wilhelm said, both of them rode roan horses with rifle scabbards on their saddles and a bedroll over the front by the pommel, they had crossed bandoliers of ammunition and broad brimmed hats against the sun and dust as they travelled across the veldt, in common with all Boer soldiers there was no uniform and they were just wearing their everyday work clothes; they both had one change of clothes packed if they were needed and they were well prepared as they set off.

They spent the next two days travelling over the veldt and retiring to the foothills and mountain slopes at night, constantly on the lookout for, and avoiding any contact, with the several patrols they had seen already in the distance.

Nights were a sad existence, unable to light a fire, for fear of revealing their location, they simply tethered the horses each night, located the Southern Cross in the night sky and confirmed their direction for the next day, ate a frugal meal of jerky washed down with cold water and tried to stay warm against the chill of the African night.

'Man there are some soldiers and supplies with those British' Wilhelm said to Louis on the second day 'Soldiers, horses,field pieces, mules and wagons, I look forward to when we meet up with a Kommando and start shaking them up a bit, as long as we stay out of their sight we will be alright'

On the third day while striking across the Veldt they saw two patrols break away from a main group of military and begin to head in their direction.

'They have spotted us and must have had outriding scouts, head for the hills' cried Louis spurring his horse with Wilhelm twisting to follow him.

To the rear one of the squad had confirmed the rising dust from their horses and the Sergeant called out 'Tally ho ! we have foxes, let's go boys'

James and Bill, two New Zealander's were a part of the squad of about twelve and were that squads only Colonial troops, recent arrivals to the front 'come on Bill' called James ' they aren't going to foot it with us, lets go , our first chance to get some Boers'.

Wilhelm and Louis had made a ravine and set off up the valley floor until they came to a sidling track that they knew of from hunting these areas years back, and they set off heading up to a ledge which would allow them to stand off any approaching opposition .

Next minute, while only a short way up but forced by terrain to move slowly, shots struck the rocks beside their mounts. 'Lord those are close, get off and get down' cried Wilhem.

Below them Bill and James had pulled to a halt and begun firing while the rest of the squad was now also entering the ravine behind them. ' that's slowed their progress' yelled Bill 'we have got them cornered now'

Meanwhile Wilhelm and Louis had moved as close to the inner edge of the track as possible, reducing the target and were leading the mounts as fast as they could up the track ' there is a bit of a hole beside the track just up here, where we can shelter and return a bit of fire' Wilhelm called, in the meantime shots were peppering the rocks all around them and the horses were rearing and having to be forcibly dragged uphill to the safety of the recess.

One of the horses fell behind them and lay dead on the track and next Louis cried out in pain but continued until suddenly they were in the recess and out of sight of the opposing forces.

'Are you alright' Wilhelm said ' where have you been shot' he asked.

'Fair in the cheek of my bum' was the retort ' luckily there is a bit of excess fat there, but it still hurts like crazy, we might be alright for a while now, I can't see them ever getting past the horse without us picking them off and at nightfall we should be able to sneak to the end of the track at the plateau above and get away, grab a sneak look over the lip of the track and see what we are up against, while I stop the bleeding and wrap my arse' Louis said 'who are those bastards, I didn't know the Brits could shoot like that'

Wilhelm carefully peered over the rim ' there are only two of them below us, taking cover near the rocks on the ravine floor, but about another ten coming fast, I think the two in front are those Colonial fellows, man they are a bit of a handful, they must have ridden like the hounds to get so far in front of the others ' he called, next minute retreating from the rim as another couple of shots raised chips from the rocks around him.

He carefully moved higher to a new vantage point and watched as the new arrivals stood in the open and called out to the first two riders he had seen, he raised his rifle and carefully sighted on one of the mounted soldiers and squeezed off a round, he saw him fall and the others wheel and start to move towards some rocks for concealment .

Wilhelm guessed a lead and followed one of the moving soldiers and squeezed off another round and was a little amazed to watch as he too fell from his mount and lay still on the ground .

In seconds there was a salvo of bullets flying around and bits of rock were flying in all directions as he retreated to the safety of the inside of the track again where he was not visible from the floor of the ravine.

Meanwhile the troops in the floor of the gorge were sheltered behind what cover they could find and calling to each other until finally one of them ventured from cover and began crawling to the second soldier that had been shot.

'Cover us' called out James leaping to his feet ' don't bother crawling, move fast and we will have a better chance' he yelled as they ran to the prone body and began to drag it to the shelter of the rocks.

The others had laid up a barrage of fire up the side of the track but there was no response from above in any event.

'Lord they must have ammunition to burn' Wilhelm said to Louis as they sheltered against the side of the track and the bank 'let's have a look at your wound and we'll sit it out until dusk and make a move'

Below them another two were running towards the other downed soldier and then rapidly dragging him as well to shelter.

'It's too late they are both gone anyway, if they even lasted after being shot' was the verdict .

'very brave to recover them but in the end risked another one or two people' their Lance Corporal voiced his opinion.'From now on we are not going to move until dusk nears and we are going to move quietly when we do !' he added.

Wilhelm was attending to Louis' wound ' you will have something to show your Grandchildren when they are old enough' Wilhelm laughed. 'it's only hit the fleshy bit and it wasn't a dum dum so should be alright, I don't know how it will be riding a horse but hopefully we will find out tonight' he added.

They spent an afternoon with Wilhelm periodically crawling to the edge of the track and checking for any movement from below but all was quiet, they had recovered Louis' gear from the dead horse and as dusk was eminent they began to lead the remaining horse up the track, all the time keeping to the inner edge to avoid being seen.

Finally they reached the plateau just on nightfall and mounted double began to head North again 'we will travel until about midnight then rest up when we should be far enough ahead of them' Wilhelm had decided and it was a compliant Louis who agreed in spite of his aching posterior!

Below and behind them as dusk neared the Lance Corporal said 'right this is how we will do it, you trooper Jones are to lead the way, the rest of you will follow providing cover if needed, we will have to move single file leading the horses, do not rush, look carefully around each corner before proceeding Jones and we will catch them tonight, do you all understand ?'

There was a muttered agreement and they set off, several minutes later Jones was several hundred feet above the floor of the gorge and rounded a corner to see the fallen horse that had been shot, as he neared it his horse began to whinny loudly and rear, Jones grabbed the bit bringing his head down when suddenly the horse reared again and swung its head viciously .

Suddenly Jones and the horse had neared the outer edge of the track Jones desperately trying to control the horse, which now, eyes rolling and snorting continuously suddenly hit a patch of loose material.

Next second they were over the edge Jones screaming as they fell, one bounce against the edge of the cliff face and then they were lying on the ground at the floor of the gorge again.

'Stop where you are, back your horses into the bank starting at the rear and go back down one at a time carefully' said the Lance Corporal.

Several minutes later, although it had seemed to take a long time, they were all back at Jones and his horse, two lifeless bodies .

'I think we have had enough of this place, we shall load our dead onto three of your mounts and three of you will have to double up, I don't know where they are headed but they are on the North side so I assume heading in that direction and we will just have to hope we or someone else can catch up with them again, they have only one horse between them so will have to slow down, we are returning to the main squadron, one round to the bastards, remember this day next time you get some of them in your sights, form up and lets go.

It was a chastened group that headed back to the main group 'Those poor Brits, nice chaps , but terrible soldiers and horsemen' said Bill in an aside to James ' I feel sorry for them, I reckon they are a bit out of their league fighting in this kind of place' was the response.

Above them on the Level Plateau Wilhelm had back sighted to the Southern Cross and they were off again heading towards the Kommando ' I hope they haven't moved too far or we won't find them but we have to hope, the sooner we are with them the better and I can rest my aching rear' said Louis. 'we did pretty well for our first engagement, a few more of those, a few thousand more of us, and they will be thinking again about buggering off and leaving us alone' he added.

That night they rested up chewing on a bit of Biltong for sustenance and taking a careful ration of water as they used some of their supply cleaning Louis' wound and the next morning they set off again ' we can't stay in the open any more and will have to make our way across the plateau and then stick to the cover of the hills and bush until we near our rendezvous' they had decided and proceeded cautiously toward the Kommando.

Two days later they are united with the Kommando led by General Christian Botha and spend a few hours recuperating and checking weapons and mounts, the force is several thousand strong and split into units with several field pieces distributed among them.

Louis sits out the next couple of weeks while his wound heals and he constantly moans at the lack of action and spends some time hunting for game to feed the increasing demands for and shortage of food.

Over the next few weeks Wilhelm is with a unit and they are alternately striking at the Empire forces generally by 'blowing' the rail tracks at strategic locations, peppering the troops accompanying the train with the Maxim machine guns then fleeing to the safety and sanctuary of the hills or trekking to new locations and planning other strategies.

He has impressed his fellows with his clear thinking and hands on attitude to learning new skills especially with explosives and generally assisting in most actions and within the first two weeks he has been asked to be, and promoted to, a Sergeant.

He has had a fair bit of comment when he arrives back at the camp and again catches up with Louis 'lord look what happens when you go away for a couple of weeks, give you a couple of months and you will be a General' scoffs Louis

'A rank in this army can be a pretty transient thing' Wilhelm replies 'upset a couple of the others and you are voted out again, and it's not as if we are getting paid for it!'

Secretly they are both pretty amused by the new rank and enjoying one anothers company again.

The main force has some of the gold reserves in wagons and are making their way towards Machadorp to try and make contact with forces and obtain more ammunition but they are being harried by Empire troops in all directions and have been forced to find their way through and then evade the forces massing to begin the great drive.

The war stretches on de Wet who had made his way to the south and Cape Colony has lost all his field guns and is in retreat and in February 1902 he will have Kitchener's forces in hot pursuit towards the Vet River .

In May 1901 de la Rey has been defeated near Ventersdorp and generally things are going poorly for the Boer forces as they enter another Winter and they are almost locked in small bands throughout the mountainous areas for sanctuary and shelter.

Game is becoming hard to find and its often dangerous to hunt as shots seem to attract attention and Empire forces reaction each time they try

Wilhelm received news via the grapevine that Marie and his children are all dead in the concentration camps and he sobs the night he receives the news receiving comfort from Louis but becoming even more embittered and full of hatred for the British forces.

Into 1902 and they know that overtures for peace have begun in February but been rejected and they are reduced to poor specimens, their original clothes and boots have all worn out after being patched as much as possible and their garb is similar to many others a combination of old salvaged rags, supplemented with bits of strategic animal skins, boots taken from dead soldiers both their own and the enemy and a miscellany of hats of all types and shapes.

Their patrols now are reduced to small roving bands trying to harass the enemy but more often than not failing and being continually hounded back into the hills and ravines.

Early in June 1902 they have been sent out together to reconnoitre the surrounding veldt and see if they can locate any enemy movements and ascertain the strength of them

They are unaware that the war has in fact been over now for 4 days and a treaty signed at Vereeniging on 31st May by the Boer commanders de la Rey, Botha and de Wet

Louis and Wilhelm have been together but separated near mid morning to unite again at evening and Wilhelm has seen a patrol of about six soldiers some kilometres distant, he has spent a bit of time setting out piles of stones and cob from the wreckage of a farm as range definition markers and has retired to the refuge of a kopje about 500 metres distant and perhaps another 2 kilometres to the mountains.

He lies there hidden in what slight scrub there is and sees the patrol approach with one of the soldiers in the lead and waits as the enemy nears his 500 metre pile and Wilhelm prepares to take a shot.

Chapter 9 : The Combatants – For Great Britain

Charles Neville Blaker – a South African Scot.

Port Elizabeth 11th December 1899

Readers Note : This chapter content is drawn from the Diary and my research (see precis)

Charles Blaker was a young man of 25 years old and living in Port Elizabeth South Africa, his Scottish family had emigrated to the continent and he was working as an office worker on this day.

Port Elizabeth, situated in the Eastern Cape province was a city that enjoyed pleasant climate, beautiful beaches and had been founded in 1820. It had been called the 'Liverpool of South Africa' as it was a major British Port and a transit point for troops discharging from ships and then heading to the front by rail.

He recalled as a youth seeing Brunell's Great Eastern with its distinctive four masts and the largest ship in the world sailing past outside the Port and he had been told the story of when a black youth Erasmus Jacobs in 1867, while playing, had kicked a bright stone and found a pretty rock; the start of the worlds largest Diamond reserves and then as a 12 year old when George Harrison an Australian Miner had discovered Gold near Johannesburg *(although there had been previous Gold finds prior to this event this was the significant find and led to the Witwatersrand gold reef and George was richly rewarded selling the claim for the princely sum of ten pounds! He was recognized as the British wished to ensure the credit fell to the Anglo sector of the population! Amazing history for the worlds richest reserves)*

During his youth the Port was often visited by sailing ships and many battled the South East gales common on the coast and there were many failures with the North End beach being strewn with wrecks, he had witnessed some of the shipwrecks and remembered the frantic efforts of the Rocket Brigade and the Life Boats attempting to rescue the crews.

He had also remembered a joke against the Port by one of the Rand Newspapers who had reported the shipping news:

Passed the Port	Nil
Arrivals	Nil
In the River	Nil
Departures	Nil

"Nil Desperandum" *(even I can see the humour in the reporting nearly a 150 years later)*

In contrast during the early stages of the war he had seen the Port crowded with ships including 42 sailing ships,51 steamers and 2 warships anchored at one time.

Charles must have had a wry humour and considered his race as being ever ready to fight for Justice, and his diary records 'when there was nothing to fight we fought among ourselves', he recalled a joke when an Irishman had happened on two men fighting and who when they rested had asked 'is this a private fight or can anyone join in?'

During the week of this day he had heard of the British defeats during the Boer war at Stormberg and Colenso, all in spite of the cheering on for their forces as they had been landing and departing for the front, he was shocked to hear of the significant defeat at Magersfontein when he had called in to the paper office on his way home from work and learned of the terrible losses and the disaster to the Highland Brigade, the Scottish Regiment.

Magersfontein was situated South of Kimberley and was near the border with Orange Free State and Cape Colony, the battle had been between a force of near 15,000 British troops, including Australians, Canadians, The Black Watch, Highland Brigade, Grenadier Guards and many other battalions fighting a force of about 10,000 Boers led by General Cronje.

The Boers had entrenched fortifications and installed barbed wire defence lines in two rows atop a raised area of ground. The British had begun their battle by an artillery barrage for two hours then a series of advances towards the Boers marching in formation with groups of 100 soldiers holding a rope between them and in lines with six paces behind them another line of 100 and so on. As they neared the Boer barbed wire entanglements they hit a number of trip wires and tin cans which alerted the Boer to their approach and position.

With their cries of 'Through God and the Mauser' the Boers fired at the massed troops trying to breach the barbed wire and a slaughter was the result, nevertheless frontal attacks in regimented lines was a British tradition and needless to say further lines were ordered into the carnage and it was a disaster for the British when they finally were forced to abandon the attack with major losses.

The war correspondent Arthur Conan Doyle had reported the Highland Brigade suffering 700 casualties in the first 7 minutes! There was pause at the cessation of the fighting when the two forces recovered their dead and injured and at the close of the battle there had been 902 British dead compared to 236 Boer. The British Commander was discharged and never took part in any future battles and all considered it was the end of a disastrous week for the British army.

The week would in future be called the 'Black Week'and many had considered it a bad omen before the battle which was fought on a Sunday, a desecration of the Holy day!

On the next morning Charles walked the street to work with three of his friends and as they passed the recruiting office they 'left wheeled' as one with a general laugh and held council as to which "crowd' they should join. By 9:30 that morning they had all enlisted.

Charles went to his Boss and told him what he had done and recalled the sad look on his face as he had just lost a son-in-law at the battle of Grasspan, nevertheless he wished Charles a safe return.

They were instructed to leave that day and to dress in old clothes and to travel to Cradock, 1st class on the train where they would be made "pretty" in their new Khaki, they would be paid 5 bob (shillings) a day and found. On that first night the train pulled up at a siding and they were given a blanket and told to 'doss down' in a Saleyards. At this point no uniforms had been issued and a multitude of dress types and colours plus Bowlers, Caps, Straw Hats etc. were worn as most lay down in the sheep pens, in the morning when they rose all were covered in a reddish dust and presented a pretty scruffy example of an army!

It was 4 days later when they finally reached Cradock and in total there was 112 men who had joined the Cape Mounted Rifles 78th Company, they had minimal training and called themselves the 'Rough Riders' *(Readers note: there was a plethora of 'Rough Riders' from all corners of the globe adopting a name made famous and first coined by Theodore Roosevelt and generally applied to troops with little formal training)*

Two days later and they had been outfitted and issued with their rifles and bayonets to open 'Bully beef' tins and had made camp establishing a tent camp, digging latrines and taking turns as cooks, which was a bit of a disaster until Charles had found an old Native who had done his cooking for him; after the meal and the congratulations he told what he had done and he was commandeered as their permanent cook. They had received further training and passed a test where they all received the 'Gren Ribbon' awarded after they had ridden a wooden bucking horse although one of their troop had done the test twice, once for himself and then under another name for his pal who they had thought would need glue and sticking plaster to pass for himself!

In February 1900 they had been inspected and a number selected for Scout duties, these were soldiers able to speak a modicum of Dutch and Kaffir and Charles and his 3 mates were all part of this group and they were cheered out of the camp as they set off for their new task to assist General French at the Modder River. They were all lapsed into silence as they left each wrapped in his own thoughts, none knowing who would be called and not return, but within a few miles they were again discussing the general advance and the soon to be, termination of the dreadful war!

In true military precision they were diverted from their original destination to travel to Thebus and aid General Erasmus who in Charles words was 'fooling about in that area' and they spent two days with his forces.

One of their force named Smith was placed on guard duty the night before they left and had called out 'Halt who goes there?' three times and then discharged his rifle resulting in the 5000 assembled men rising from their beds in the early morn and beginning to form up and saddle horses and lower tents for an advance.

It was a chagrined group of Scouts who departed the next morning to assist General French, a matter of some urgency by now, but again they were diverted this time to Arundel siding where the Boers were engaged in shelling that camp. They felt very keenly that they were not keeping their appointment with the Commander-in Chief and asked their Sergeant to send him their best wishes and to 'get on with it' as they were busy. To their amazement he did and the message was received.

At Arundel they had their first baptism of fire, at 2:00 am a force of 75 of their troops were ordered to escort 2 field guns to the artillery camp a few miles distant and then to open 'negotiations' with the opposing forces! Just on Dawn the opposition was discovered and heavy rifle fire broke out and their 2 guns began firing with horsemen racing for cover until their Officers told them to 'Stand fast' Charles recalled he didn't know what that meant until they were all sitting astride their horses, smoking and watching the action though their field glasses. He was curious at the little spurts of dust rising from the ground and the bees passing in a hurry until he was told 'Bullets you ---- fool' , he stated that a dreadful feeling came over him as he felt 75 men standing must have presented a good target and they stood for 20 minutes although no one has hurt and, in fact, several 12 pound segment shells had also passed across their lines!

In his words when the order to move was issued not a man hesitated and a better 75 jockies would not have been found not even at the Classic Steeple Chase Meetings, as they tore off in an arc to take up another position facing the enemy and began a counter attack.

He also said that one of their number a youth of 17 had misunderstood the order and ridden back to camp where he was immediately placed in the Guard Tent and accused of desertion! Although he was treated sympathetically by the Officers the incident shattered him and he wept that he could never face his Mother again, he would have preferred he had been killed and bore a shamed life, Charles finally lost touch with him and never knew how his life turned out after that!

Charles war continued and they finally left Arundel to receive an order that General French wanted 50 picked men and horses with knowledge of Dutch and Kaffir to ride stripped saddles with 2 days provisions and thence to live off the country to leave at 2:30 am and thence to call at Colesburg Junction for further orders. It was with pride and the envy and good wishes of his fellows that they set off on a dangerous mission to help win the war. Again Charles was to be disillusioned, they arrived at Colesburg Junction to be told that no one knew anything about them and that they had better wait for orders, 32 days later with no tent, blanket, pot or cooking utensils they were still waiting! To fill in time they did patrols and acted as telegraph orderlies etc, but the difficulty was the cooking until they were adopted? by the Argyle Militia who cooked meals for them and generally looked after them.

Still thinking that there specialist force of 75 were urgently wanted somewhere they grumbled to their Officers and threatened to go without leave and one of the men was sent to convey the case to the Officer-in-Command. The Tommies filled him with drink after he had put the case and was preparing to return and he was full of this as he sighted an out post of the shifting head quarters of the army and thinking it was the enemy engaged them sprinkling the picket with nickel! Instead of returning as a hero he was incarcerated in the main camp as a prisoner, however, on the following day orders were received to rejoin the main force at Donkerpoort and their miscreant soldier was also released to accompany them.

The force proceeded generally North until they reached a railway bridge at Norvalls Point, this was a pontoon bridge built after the permanent structure had been destroyed only to be told they had signed up under 'the Colonial Act' and they had to return and camp on the right bank (on the Cape Colony side!) It was discovered after about 2 days they were actually on the wrong bank so they crossed the river again and set up camp yet again. Patrols and swimming in the river was not what they had come to the war for and there were further threats of rebellion until their Commander decided he would establish another Scout company with a new set of Volunteers, to no ones amazement every one of them re-volunteered and several days later they were on the move towards Bloemfontein in high glee leaving behind a camp guard of 12 of which Charles was one being incapacitated.

His duties consisted of keeping everyone happy and attend on the Commandant and acquire various items from the numerous trains in the form of cases of Whisky, boxes of Cigarettes and got a taste for 'Flag' cigarettes which he described as the best and purest going-no adulteration-everything in such as bits off string, splinters of wool, pieces of finger nail etc.

In due course the camp guard packed up and went to Bloemfontein and rejoined his fellow squad of volunteers, in spite of having no kit and supplies they camped for another 2 days until Lord Roberts visited and enquired how they were? On being told the sad plight he instructed tents be arranged for them and supplies and actually waited until they were delivered.

The war continued and Charles went to Dewets Dorp to relieve a siege but arrived too late already relieved by other columns and they spent some time rounding up stray cattle for the army.

They had watched as the Highland Brigade left in May 1901 marched out on trek and envying the Scouts who would be guarding and protecting them until it was discovered it was supposed to be their job as Cavalry, however their orders had been misplaced, and there was a mad rush as they rapidly packed up to pursue the force leaving all their food behind in the rush!

Their battles continued through Heilbron and they crossed paths with General Hamilton at Verkeerdeplaats and saw the Gordons, Black Watch and other famous regiments as they continued their scouting and other duties. Their scouting role was to ride in pairs around the columns and at least one mile from the nearest infantryman and always in touch with each other 'link', to feel the position and signal 'all clear,' to continue the advance of troops, enter any farm houses and seek information from natives etc. He remembered it as 'nervy' work always being observant of Dongas and Hillocks for that was commonly where guerrilla forces would fire from as they approached. They then had to try an establish the size of the opposing force and report to the command.

At one point the columns where held up by the combined Boer forces of de Wet, Erasmus and Prinsloo but managed to break through and continue the fight and spent considerable time near Lindley where there was strong Boer resistance. In time Charles and his troop had heard of the relief of Mafeking and the turning fortunes of the war and over a period involving many confrontations they finally ended back near Heilbron where they had started many months previously. Their section had dwindled to half through attrition and action and they were placed in houses to carry out reconnaissance duties and other scouting and seeking out and reporting on the enemy Boers and taking captive those Boers who surrendered.

Finally Charles and the remnants of the scouts were at Krugersdorp on boring Garrison duties and it was here that one of their patrols was ambushed, two of the youth that Charles had volunteered with were killed, one with his back broken by a bullet and the other with nine bullets in his body, both shot at a range of less than 20 yards. The camp was enraged and the funeral was a large affair with three trumpeters to play the 'Last Post' and a large firing party.

Again they ended up waiting around and setting off only to be recalled until they were asked if they wished to take their discharge at which time most left and were entrained to their homes, each man carrying his rifle and ammunition as an armed guard to the train and travelling in first class – 'open trucks' but with their blankets they were reasonably comfortable until they were back at Cradock and then returned to Port Elizabeth the next day.

Charles had telegraphed his sister and as he got off the train with his Greatcoat, a heavy beard, two bandoliers etc. he was unrecognised until he made himself known to her.

Charles had also met with, and commented on, some of the Australian soldiers writing ' *Hard fighters, splendid fighters with initiative and every man a leader. Great fellows in the field in the fighting line- nothing of the Drawing Room there but – I am much in sympathy with them for after all War is war.'*

His thoughts on the concentration camp were counter to many others and his words were: '*I regret to say that many of our men thought concentration camps a mistake and that the Women and Children should have been left to the care of the Boers on their farms, and that this would have brought about the end of the war earlier than it did. I can only look upon the formation of the camps as being a merciful measure – unfortunately not understood or appreciated'*

Readers note: this chapter is a summary of the extensive diary notes I was privileged to read and there are many other anecdotes and memories including details of a court martial and what we would regard as pretty harsh treatment of one Native in particular, signs of a different time. The chapter is appended as a true record of one mans experiences in the war representing the English people of South Africa at the time.

Chapter 10 : The Combatants – for England

Tommy Jones

London East End 1901

London's East end was a sad place to live and die, it had been the subject of Charles Dickens books with an underlying plea for social reform and Jack London, the Author had written :

--- *'it is incontrovertible that that the children grow up into rotten adults, without vitality or stamina, a week kneed, narrow chested, listless breed that crumples up and goes down in the struggle for life'*-----

Tommy Jones was 16 years old and was one of the countless 'pound a week', or often less!, poor in the biggest City in the World.

He was a victim of the poverty and squalor which permeated the city where Cholera, Tuberculosis and other diseases were rife among the poor, where there were few communal wash houses to attend on personal hygiene and clothes washing and the permanent stink of the effluent from the hundreds of horses that used the streets and the Butchers and Fish shops in particular was almost continuously in the air.

Tommy sought out casual work where he could which varied from working in the 'sweated industries' of the garment business in unventilated factories or on the gangs of labourers constantly required for the arduous work in the construction of the 'Bazelgettes' sewer system which was to change the face of the city.

While the latter was often extremely uncomfortable work it at least gave Tommy some measure of strength and while the fetid air of the trenches was not conducive to good health the times walking to the sites and afterwards sitting in some of the better air in the city meant that he enjoyed some little measure of health.

So it was as the Boer War entered its second year and there was a lack of numbers of troops in the British army the War Office began a recruiting spree for the Imperial Yeomanry. In contrast to the earlier recruitment they now included people of the working class and Tommy had decided maybe this was an opportunity for him to escape the slums and poverty of his London home and see a bit of the world while getting paid for it.

He had heard that the Boers were virtually finished and he was keen to see if he could get in to the army and overseas before the scrap was over.

Readers note: seven out of every nine recruits from London slums were rejected from service and large numbers sent home after arrival in South Africa as unsuitable for the army!

He duly presented himself at the recruiting station where there were quite strict requirements regarding weight, height, strength and others which he managed to pass and was advised 'we are going to turn you into mounted infantry, I know you know nothing about horsemanship or marksmanship but we are going to give you plenty of training and turn you into good British soldiers, what do you say to that' he was asked.

'Sounds good to me' was his response

'Sir!' the officer almost screamed 'you are within minutes of being inducted, you horrible little man, we are also going to teach you about discipline and stature and your Mother will be proud of you when we are finished or else you are not going to enjoy yourself, do I make myself understood?'

'Yes I understand thank you'

This time the response was almost apoplectic as the officer screamed at the top of his voice 'sir! get it!'

A contrite Tommy said 'yes Sir' standing as tall as he could and was duly inducted into the army.

Within a few days the new soldiers had been issued with uniforms, and assembled into some semblance of order, and to the strains of the popular tune 'Dolly Gray' shuffled off to the waiting trains to take them to the port for embarkation to South Africa.

I have come to say goodbye Dolly Gray

It's no use to ask me why Dolly Gray

There's a murmer in the air, you can hear it everywhere

It's the time to do and dare Dolly Gray

As they boarded the train to the cheers and tearful farewells of the crowd, the flag waving and the sense of being part of a great Army moved Tommy to reflect on his future.

'it's a great and glorious thing to fight for England in her hour of need' he remembered someone saying and his chest swelled with pride

The new British Commander Kitchener had decided in his wisdom that they should be 'Trained-in-Theatre' and accordingly they were on their way to South Africa within a fortnight of his enlistment.

Tommy joined the rest of his new friends in being seasick for the first few days of the voyage and the derision of the crew; while their formal training was to take place in South Africa they received training in how to look after their mounts in the holds of the ships, a location which didn't help their tender stomachs at all.

After several soldiers had been bitten by, or had their foot stood on by a horse, and after their initial dismay at how large and fearful they were they began to establish some kind of rapport and understanding of the beasts, of course they had observed them around the streets of their home and avoided the excreta which covered most of the pavements however actually being in control of the animals was a new experience for virtually all of them.

They were also introduced to their new weaponry, not for them the new Lee Enfield rifles instead they were issued the older Martini Henry 'falling block' single shot 577/450 lever action rifles and learned the intricacies of maintenance and cleaning and drilled on the deck to learn some basics and skills and attempted to learn how to sight and fire their rifles at drogues towed behind the ship. They were told 'if you can't shoot better than that I don't give much hope for your chances' after several hundred rounds of ammunition had been fired with scarcely more than a few hits on the target!

Finally they landed in South Africa and were entrained again to travel North towards Pretoria and on arrival began their 'Trained-in-Theatre' instruction; after the first day when several of the soldiers had been either unable to mount their horses, traveling round and round as the steeds refused to stand still, or were thrown off ungraciously even if they were able to get into the saddle; their frustrated Sergeants and Corporals were wringing their hands together asking 'what have we done to deserve this' and 'how on earth are these ever going to be able to move let alone fight'

Rifle training was suffering the same with many of the troops unable to even aim correctly, recoiling and flinching at the recoil of the heavy rifles and some even unable to score anything on the range as a result of completely missing the targets a repetition of their efforts on the ship .

Tommy had been with the second contingent which had nearly sixteen thousand men when it had left England but by the end of the first month over seven hundred were on their way back to England and would be discharged as 'unsuitable for duty'.

The Imperial Yoeman were not highly regarded Tommy was discovering to his chagrin and were the victims of scorn and abuse from several other detachments including all the Colonial forces including New Zealanders, Australians, Canadians, Indians and even their own battalions.

The first contingent although of a finer breeding and stock had suffered several defeats in every battle they had been involved in and were given the nickname by some *'de Wets own'* because of the significant numbers of horses, rifles and ammunition they were losing to the enemy.

Tommy was finally able to ride his horse although he always had trouble with it when it adopted an recalcitrant mood and it tended to go around in circles to his annoyance and he was constantly being reminded to 'let up on the bit' and 'hold the reins loose' and 'try and go in one direction you horrible little man' to the amusement and rankling of other troops watching on.

The troops had assembled with other battalions at Pietersburg to begin a 'push' of the Boers towards the east and the waiting British Blockades and barbed wire and in the interim a number of patrols were being sent out to check and report on possible Boer activity in the area.

Several of the Imperial Yeomanry were being accompanied by Australian or New Zealand soldiers in the hope that some of their skills would rub off onto the hapless troops as they saw how 'it should be done' and Tommy had ended up in a squad with two New Zealanders who evidenced exactly those skills when they sighted two Boers in the distance and the squad gave chase.

The New Zealanders were leading every one else and pursued the Boer into a ravine and Tommy could hear the sounds of firing as the following troops rode into the ravine.

'We think we have hit one of them and they have skedaddled up that sidling track' they pointed out from near some rocks as the others milled about, suddenly there was a shot from above and one of Tommy's mates fell to the ground and they rushed to cover as a second shot rang out and another trooper fell from the saddle.

The afternoon was spent resting up although the two bodies, both dead, had been retrieved under the cover of a fusillade of shots to where it was thought the enemy was hiding.

Later in the day it is decided to follow the Boer up the track and try to attack them and Jones is selected to lead the advance and his horse.

All the while he is thinking 'this isn't how I thought the war was going to be, the sooner this is over the better'

He advances up the track carefully and rounds a corner and meets a dead horse lying in front of them.

His mount begins to snort and rear and he is frantically trying to control and calm it when suddenly it nears the outer edge of the track which collapses under its weight and it begins to fall over the edge and Tommy Jones goes with it!

Chapter 11 : The Combatants – for Australia

David O'Reilly and John Murphy

Ballarat Victoria Australia 1887

It was a hot summers day and behind the School buildings ten year old David was learning the hard way about prejudice and religious doctrines as he was being beaten up by the school bully.

'When you see me again get out of my way you bloody catholic spud eater, my dad says you micks are all the same' was the message being delivered along with the hiding as a result of his walking along in a bit of a dream when he had bumped into the bully.

As he lay on the ground surrounded by the other children another figure leapt forward 'don't you dare speak of us like that' cried out John as he advanced on the bully with fists raised.

Within a few seconds he had joined David on the ground with a badly bleeding nose and their tormentor was walking away accompanied by his sneering mates.

'Well that didn't work' said David as they rose shakily to their feet 'but thanks for trying to help me out, even if we had both gone at him at once I think we might have still had a beating, the protty bastard'

'We'll get him one day, just maybe not today, in fact he might be safe for a while' said John and they both began laughing.

So began a friendship forged in adversity, well sort of, which lasted as they grew up.

Their school days were marked by a series of disparaging remarks especially from the bully and they bided their time but unfortunately never achieved any measure of revenge, in fact received several more beatings over the years in spite of an ingrained Irish propensity for a scrap their noble aspirations were doomed to failure.

They lived in a couple of houses in the lower part of town and both their Fathers were mine workers.

Ballarat was a city in the Colony of Victoria in Australia in the central highlands, the discovery of alluvial gold in 1857 and the rich fields had bought tens of thousands to 'the Golden city' which had peaked at a population of about sixty thousand before settling back to about twenty three thousand which was its current population. The ready supply of alluvial gold had 'dried up' and deep underground mining by large companies was required for extraction.

Both David and Johns parents had emigrated from and after chasing another gold dream in California with a view to making it rich, but like many before them had found that this dream only seemed to be realised by a lucky few.

For some weekends they often continued to fossick and the boys accompanied them with their other siblings and learnt how to divert watercourses, build weirs, construct sluice boxes, wash up and pan for gold, build and operate 'rockers' when water was hard to get and how to shovel and shift tons of the earths gravels for little reward; in other words how to be a failed gold miner but still kept trying waiting for the one big strike that would change everything.

The one thing that all this did was build up their bodies and strength, they also learnt how to drink, a valuable Irish trait, as was an inability to control it sometimes and they also had the Irish love of a good scrap with varied results.

By thirteen they had both left school, there was a large Irish community in the city and they spent time in the bush to the North, South and South West learning the ways of the bush and hunting wild pigs, kangaroos, wetland birds and anything else that moved which they sold around the area butchered and dressed up for the table. They had learned how to use the wind to their favour when stalking and how to approach quietly through the bush and scrub and even out in the open, where it was possible to approach game by a series of small movements and stopping each time the animal raised its head to look around.

They had acquired an old Martini Henry falling block single shot rifle, a Winchester .22 rifle and a double barrelled shotgun which they have become quite proficient at using.

An old bushman had shown them a bit of navigation for when they became 'bushed' at night and especially how to locate the 'Southern Cross'. 'you have to find the two pointers then find the group of bright stars, then extend the main side of the cross by four and a half times its length and this points to the south pole' they were taught 'you can call it a kite with a tail five times longer than the kite if you like with the pole at the end of the tail!'

They have continued a life of living in the bush and spending their time hunting and selling the processed game, their other alternative is to join the band of underground miners working the big gold claims but they prefer the outdoors. However, they are now in their early twenties and getting restless feet and trying to decide if they should move to somewhere new for a bit of adventure. They have no commitments, finding romance, or all they need anyway with the plentiful ladies of the night that frequent certain areas of the City after dark.

In 1899 the Boer war has broken out and one day they decide maybe we join the Colonial Army to see the world, have a secure job with possibly a bit of excitement thrown in to the mix and so they visit a recruitment office, which has been set up for just that reason in the centre of town

'You need to be good shots, good riders, 20 to 40 years old, over 5foot 6inches and with a chest measurement over 34 inches and pass a medical, looks like you qualify for everything except the medical so far, I take it you can ride' the recruiting officer asked.

'Too bloody right mate' John responded 'but we don't have our own horses just now, lost them in a bet' he added

'The army will supply everything you need' said the officer and he began to note their details and arranged for a medical towards the end of that week.

'How are we going to learn to ride a bloody horse' said David 'They might be bit different to our old mule we lead to carry game!'

'No sweat there's a couple in a paddock behind our house we just need to catch them and teach ourselves it can't be very hard, I have seen lots of them and watched people, looks bloody simple to me' was the response.

That was the first mistake, try as they might they couldn't even catch one of the horses to try a bit of bareback riding, the first time they got at all close one of the horses had bit David, to his dismay and he was considering chucking this in!

After about 20 minutes they were interrupted by a voice asking 'what do you think you are doing with my horses' and the owner walked towards them, he was greatly amused when they told him they had to be good riders before they could join the army but then spent some time introducing them to the animals, their traits and the tack to ride them before teaching them how to mount and ride around the paddock and then dress down the horses after exercise with a promise he would teach them a bit more and he spent several days until they had the rudiments of horsemanship and even looked like they knew what they were doing!

They were good students but still were not practiced horsemen when they had completed their medical and began training in earnest, now they were in the company of other horsemen their deficiencies became obvious but with the help of their fellow recruits and an understanding Sergeant they became a little more practiced before it was time to say goodbye to their families after two months training and load their mounts to the train that would take them to Brisbane and then via steamer to South Africa.

They spent the next year in a series of structured battles with the Boers attacking field guns and troops and were present when Mafeking was relieved and near the end of their one years service the war had almost run its course, the Orange Free State had ceded defeat and Transvaal was not far behind 'do you want to re enlist for another year' they were asked.

'I reckon this place isn't too bad, there must be gold left here, lets chuck the army and have a go before we decide what to do next, I have had enough of being a soldier' and with that the die was cast and they served out the balance of their time and set off as gold prospectors and miners in the Transvaal near Rustenburg where they began searching along with a few others for the elusive mineral!

A year later and the war is still going on albeit now a guerrilla war by the Boers and their only legacy so far was a series of holes all over the countryside which had been checked out and then discarded as possible 'el doradoes', they where actually even more broke than when they had left the army.

While they worked hard they also played hard and bore a few bruises and scratches from their last night out, unfortunately cut short by two factors, the first when they ran out of money and credit and the second when they were thrown unceremoniously out into the street following yet another beer inspired scrap.

'I don't know about this country' David had said when finally they staggered back to their camp and dropped into the sacking and branch beds in their shanty 'we seem to be getting a bit of a name, we don't have two bob to rub together and who won that scrap anyway ?'

'Yes I am getting a bit tired of this, that pompous prick Kitchener reckons we should form an Australian Militia and join the scrap again, at least we will get a regular pay, be able to finish off a few Boers and get them out of our hair when we go back to our gold mining' David said 'lets go and join up, apparently they only want a couple of hundred, the wars nearly over what do you say?'

'Talk to me in the morning' was the mumbled response through bruised lips!

David again broached the subject after another fruitless morning where they hadn't even struck colour in a single 'washup', 'give some thought to my idea last night about joining up and getting some regular pay and a bit of fun'

Throwing down his shovel was John's response 'bugger the gold mining, bugger giving any thought to it, lets go right now, this minute' Suddenly he picked up the shovel again and with a yell that summated all of his frustrations and anger threw the shovel into the adjacent scrub and began walking to their shanty, as he neared the door he gave a mighty kick which lifted it off its flimsy hinges and then began to leap about 'bastard thing has broken my toe' he screamed and began to jump all over the now supine door.

After cooling down a bit and after a cuppa tea they discussed a bit more quietly their options.

Like many another before them, seized by a gold fever, they were discovering that it was easy to dream of a fortune by finding gold but a bit harder to put into practice and they had been digging up parts of the Northern Transvaal for nearly a year now and in spite of digging enough soil for several hundred good gardens they had virtually no success to show for their efforts.

They called at the recruiting station for the 'Bushveldt Carbineers' and said 'we want to join your merry band'

The Australian Colonel who was bringing the concept to reality, R W Lineham looked them over 'you look like a couple of hard men or is that just an illusion, you seem to bear the marks of a good hiding and a recent battle, am I right ?' 'This is going to be a proper force of specialist Australians although we will be under British control we will be expected to be able to act by ourselves if needed and we don't need any loser larrikins' he added.

'We are pretty sure we won as a matter of fact, if you want to see if we are hard or not, find someone to step outside and try his hand at a bit of bareknuckle, loser the first who can't toe the line anymore !' was the retort. 'we have already had one year in the Army so we are just what you need'

'I am not here to arrange boxing matches, are you sure you want to join the Bushveldt Carbineers, have you got rifles, ammunition and horses or do we have to supply them as well?' he asked.

'Mate we have nothing but our strength and ability, we can both shoot and fight as well as any man and we just want our chance to prove it, your new force won't know what's struck it if you enlist us' John said 'I speak for us both, the answer to your prayers for top fighters'

The idea for the Bushveldt Carbineers had been Kitcheners, he couldn't ignore the great example of other Aussie troops; after the siege of Brakfontein last August where 300 Aussies and 200 Rhodesians have held off over 3000 Boers and 11 days of attack with over 2500 shells thrown at them the Commander of the Boers Koos de la Rey had said '*for the first time we are fighting against men who used our own tactics against us. They were Australian volunteers and although small in number we could not take their position. They were the only troops who could scout our lines at night and kill our sentries while killing or capturing our scouts. Our men admitted the Australians were formidable opponents and far more dangerous than any other British troops'.*

Lineham explained the history above which had resulted in the formation of the new force and added 'the force is being funded from the Empire coffers not our Australian funds so we can outfit you to be repaid from your wage until the debt is cleared, they will supply the horses and tack which you can keep, the rifles as well will be yours after you have paid for them, what do you say?'

'Suits us, we might have been here a couple of years but we are still Aussies and know how to scrap and we have banged a few Boer heads together already' was the response 'where do we sign?'

The process didn't take long, none of this medical stuff for these volunteers, they were all hard looking and physically strong types selected and within the month three hundred and twenty had been picked and started drilling and training..

It must be conceded the drilling would not pass muster for the rest of the British army but it was sufficient for the hard, independent men who had been picked and they did reach some sort of order and discipline. They made no acknowledgement of, and were independent of British Officers except to receive instructions as to their next role.

They were supplemented by two Australian Aboriginal trackers, part of a total of fifty who had come from Australia, again at Kitcheners' request, another of his great ideas.

The unanimous consensus was that the Aboriginals should stay separate from the other troopers, they would be provided with food and clothing plus a tent and could keep their own company until required. Their presence was acknowledged as maybe of assistance in pursuing rebels but they had no place in the company of white soldiers except when they were performing those duties and for the rest of the time they could look after themselves!

Readers Note : It is not known whether any of the Aboriginal trackers ever returned to Australia which at that time had a white Australia policy which meant they were ineligible to be returned to their homeland

By March 1901 the Carbineers were part of a force of 1300 mustered at Pretoria with General Plummer in a column to take Pietersburg, their role was to strike out and attack and subdue the Boer Kommandos who were attacking the railway instillations.

On some of the operations David and John who had stayed together were commanded by 'Breaker' Morant another ex gold miner and they were relentless in their pursuit of Boer raiders 'Kitchener has told us "Take no Prisoners" any Boer in Khaki is to be shot as well' he had told them.

'This seems a little superfluous to me ! take no prisoners means just that!' Morant said and accordingly all Boers captured were promptly shot whether in Khaki or not.

David and John weren't too comfortable with this, some of the Boers they had been mining with had been reasonable fellows and some had even joined the British forces, however, they went along with the general mood of the war, which seemed to be a continued frustration and anger by Kitchener that the Boers wouldn't simply stop fighting.

The war was continuing and getting more and more bitter with each day, the British Press and Parliament were starting to take umbrage at Kitcheners scorched earth policies and especially the Concentration Camps policy.

Emily Hobhouse had visited the Concentration camps and had prepared a scathing report on conditions at the Bloemfontein camps where the inmates because of a shortage of tents had been sleeping on the ground in the open even when pouring with rain .

She had been particularly incensed at the deaths of young children in the camps from starvation, pneumonia and diseases including typhoid,dysentery and cholera where large numbers of women and children were dying in the camps and bereft of a proper Christian burial .

Kitchener had called her 'that bloody woman', the Press had called her a traitor when her first report 'Report of a visit to the Camps of Women and Children in the Cape and Orange River Colonies' was presented but even they were now beginning to respond to public opinion and shame, and try as they might to defend the policy the Conservative Government led by the Marquess of Salisbury was becoming unable to silence the critics, the Liberal MP had told an audience

'A phrase often used is 'war is war' , but when one comes to ask about it one is told that no war is going on, that it is not war. When is a war not a war?. When it is carried on by methods of barbarism in South Africa'

Morants response to the criticism was similar to Kitchener 'break the bastards and it will be over, I don't know how they bloody stick it out, why don't they just throw in the towel and give up, these bleeding hearts don't help anything!' he espoused when asked and sometimes just volunteered to let people know where he stood on the subject .

Morant espoused Kitcheners ideal soldier and accordingly those in the know had elevated him to the rank of Lance Corporal.

Independent of all the politics and infighting David and John continued their role and were with some two hundred other members of the Carbineers riding on patrol along the main line to Pretoria some weeks later when they sighted smoke and then heard a series of explosions and a field gun firing in the distance.

The force broke into a gallop and rushed along the line until they came upon a train which had been derailed, there was a force of Boers who had blown the line derailing the train which was carrying British reserves towards Pretoria and were in the process of firing a carriage mounted Gatling gun at the carriages and troops who were frantically seeking cover.

As the relieving force approached the Gatling gun suddenly stilled, its 300 rounds a minute from the 10 barrelled gun had rapidly depleted the available ammunition and the Boers were now restricted to rifle fire and were beginning to retreat in the face of the increased resistance.

The Gatling and carriage was abandoned as the now Mounted Boers and several wagons were fleeing towards the safety of the adjacent mountains about a mile distant from the tracks.

David and John were in an advance group and the two of them began to chase down a wagon frantically being driven at speed and with the horses being lashed to try to escape while the others were chasing other groups which were dispersing in all directions to try escape.

Riding alongside the wagon David pulled out his revolver and at almost point blank range fired at the driver. The wagon veered to the side and then struck a hole in the ground and catapulted to a halt in a burst of dust and the screaming of the horses. David and John saw that the driver had been killed almost instantly and after dismounting despatched the other dazed Boer with a shot to the head and then despatched the horses.

'Lordy me, we have struck gold' yelled David to John 'look at it' he cried while watching for any of the others. Fortunately they were distant from them and they were all otherwise engaged.

'There's a fortune her , Gold several ingots, and a heap of Pound notes, quick bury them and fire the wagon' he said and they frantically buried it beneath the remains of one of the wheels and fired the wagon above the site.

Their sergeant rode up shortly as they were standing puffing on a Wills cigarette each and observing the blaze 'I see you have got them both, since when did we start a policy of cremating the enemy, was there anything of value with the wagon before you decided to burn it?' he asked

'Just old clothes and a few supplies' was the response.

'Leave it and lets get out of here, we have to see how many of the troops on the train have been injured and if we can get enough mounts to get them to safety or whether we need to protect them here until we can get another train and repair the damage' was the order.

That night David and John talked while on sentry and distant from the sleeping units who were waiting for the morrow to begin moving out 'it's a dirty bastard of a war to be in and I was almost regretting joining up again but it just got a whole lot better, beats digging the bloody stuff out of the ground, do you reckon you can find the place again after its over and all died down?' David spoke.

'We are about ten miles from Wanderfontein and not far off the siding rail line and there's the Southern Cross and that hill shaped like a lovely breast with a prominent nipple is almost directly below South so I reckon we won't have too much trouble, the wreckage of the wagon must be about one mile almost due east of here, we are going to be in mate' John chortled.

'Someone up there is looking after us, won't be long now and the war will be over and we will be back then we are in clover'

Chapter 12 The Combatants – representing Canada

Richard Evans and Roger Brown

Toronto Canada 1902

Richard Kelly and Roger Byrne had grown up together in a low to middle class suburb of the city and had been best friends for as long as they could both remember, playing, fighting and schooling together. In spite of their Irish heritage they regarded themselves as English to distinguish themselves from the French speaking fraternity they often found themselves at a varying opinion of each other.

Being avid readers of the 'Toronto World' and especially the Sunday version which appealed to and was supported by what could be described as the lower classes of Toronto society they were familiar with the Boer War and Canada's proud record to date. The 'Toronto World' was published on a Saturday night but sold on a Sunday to avoid the 'Lords Day Act' of Canada which prohibited Sunday papers, a roundabout way of circumventing the law and which appealed to most residents especially those of an Irish background.

In the initial beginning of the war there had been considerable reluctance to enter the fray with the French population almost actively supporting the Boers in principle viewing British Imperialism as a threat while the English faction wishing to rally to the Empire cause with a fervour of patriotism. In due course the Parliament voted to form a volunteer force of 1000 men to enter the war and there had been large numbers of volunteers presenting themselves. The major action they had been involved in had been the Battle of Paardeberg, South of Bloemfontein where a force of 15,000 Empire troops (combined British and Canadians) had been unable to defeat a force of about 5000 Boers after 9 days of battle, finally the Canadians had mounted an attack at night on 25th February 1900 and at dawn the next day the Boers surrendered to those troops. There had been tremendous jubilation in Canada and Britain as this was the first major British victory in the War and the British Commander at that time Field Marshall Roberts had said *'Canadian now stands for bravery, dash and courage'* Needless to say after this there was a rash of Canadian youth wanting to join the conflict and share in the National pride.

Both of their parents and families had immigrated from Ireland in the 1890's and settled in Toronto where they had raised their families Richard was 20 and Roger 21 on this day and Richard was engaged to Rogers sister Isabelle a bonny lass but with a fiery temper to match her red hair and long tresses and they were to marry in August this year at the St Basils Catholic church in downtown Toronto.

Richard and Roger on this day were working in Toronto on the 'Traders Bank Building' a project which had started in 1900 and was expected to take several years to complete. At over 180 feet high this was going to be not only the tallest building in Toronto but also in the British Empire. They were working as builders labourers lining the various floors with a multitude of others as construction progressed and in spite of the numerous coal burning heaters on each floor working to capacity it was still cold inside the structure with an outside temperature of about minus 4 degrees and snow falling.

Roger volunteered while they were having their lunch 'why don't we go and join the fun in South Africa, it's got to be warmer, if we don't hurry up we won't get a chance for overseas paid travel and its only for one year anyway, what do you say ?'

'Christ what will your Ma and Isabelle say if I call off the wedding to go to a bloody war, it won't be worth living' was Richards response.

'Ah to hell with it stand up for yourself, they will wait if they have to and I will support you when you tell them, just imagine coming back to a heroe's welcome, the stories for your kids, plus absence makes the heart grow fonder, think of the reception when you come home, it's got to be a winner all round'

It was with a confident air that Richard broached the proposal to Isabelle and her Mother that evening 'You bastard, where did this stupid idea come from?' Isabelle's Mother screamed out 'I have a good mind to teach you a lesson you shan't forget, the wedding is all arranged including the church I suggest you rethink this before you are sorry, get up Father and land one on the young fool, in fact give him one for me while you're at it and a reminder not to dally with our daughters affection, well come on hurry up!' as Isabelle sobbed in the background.

Isabelle's Father did not respond and actually slumped further into his chair ' this is for the young ones to reconcile' he said 'I'll not interfere' silently adding to himself 'the lads a bit big for me to handle at my age'

Her Mother looked on in a rage 'and I see you grinning over there Roger, I suppose you have something to do with this and don't care about your sisters broken heart'

'Jesus Ma, don't involve me in it, its not my doing' as Richard now looked at him with a barely suppressed rage.

'Don't you take our Lords name in vain in this house or you can move out' raged Mother now finding another avenue to vent her spleen.

It was not until later that evening when Richard had explained all the supposed advantages of service to his country, Isabelles pending marriage to a war hero and the fact it was only a small 6 months or so delay and when he promised to return that there was reluctant although tearful acceptance.

As they walked outside before Richard went to his home he turned to Roger 'you told me you would have my back and support me in there you lying so and so'

'Arr you were doing so well no need for both of us to risk ourselves, right then lets go and see if we can get into the Army anyway in the morning' was the retort 'great stuff never doubted you would talk them round joining up should be easy after that, the hard part is over'

And so it proved and within a week they had been inducted into the 2nd Regiment of the Canadian Mounted Rifles an intake of near 900 men trained and ready to depart to arrive in South Africa in February 1902

No sooner had they arrived than they were entrained to the front and took part in what would turn out to be one of the last significant actions of the war on 31st March 1902 'the Battle of

Boschbult Farm or Harts River' near the mouth of the Vaal River. The battle was a disaster for the British troops who had begun and also for the Canadians who came to their aid, the Boers were attacking the British camp successfully and a large group of near twenty Canadians were isolated and most killed in what would be the most telling defeat of that force in the whole Canadians war.

Luckily Richard and Roger who were together were not part of that group who had been separated and killed but were still shocked at the severity of the Boer attack and relieved when they had called it off about 5:00 o'clock that night and departed the scene.

'Jesus, I didn't think it was going to be like this' said a relieved Richard 'I thought they were supposed to be beaten not dishing out a hiding like this, thank God they gave up fighting when they did, I hope the whole war isn't going to go like this!'

'Well you have to agree they are bloody good scrappers, no wonder the Brits need us and the other Colonials they are up against it all right' Roger conceded.

At the end of May the war is over the Boers having arranged a surrender and Richard and Roger are advised that they will be leaving South Africa in July and can take an extended two weeks leave before departure.

My Dearest Isabelle

Well another letter from me

The war is finally over and I must say we have had it pretty easy all things considered.

Although we really only saw one major action we feel we are true soldiers of Canada and we have done our country and the Empire proud.

We are both unscathed by the experience and expect to be returning in July and have two weeks leave so Roger and I are going for a bit of a look around and heading towards Wanderfontein a city to the East before we return.

I look forward eagerly to our return and completing our nuptials and the day you are my wife

All my love to you and your family

Fondly   Richard

Chapter 13 : Representing the Non Combatants and the Victims

Marie

Transvaal near Wonderfontein

2nd April 1901

Marie was sweeping the stoep of the house and Millie was dressing the children while Mason tended to the chickens and Pigs, it was now 3 days since Wilhelm had ridden away and already she was lonely and missed him.

Marie was a strong , stocky woman. Her face was calm but had the furrows normal with someone who had spent much of her life squinting into the sun or worrying about her family, she remembered her Mother who had anguished the same when her Father had left for the first Boer war nearly twenty years ago, how she had cried when he never returned and how her Mother had retreated into a world of her own until her premature death some years ago .

Marie and Wilhelm had lived on her late Fathers Farm since, raising cattle, chickens for eggs and food, and Pigs to eat the waste and provide Pork and Ham and cattle for meat and hides.

They had a well stocked garden which Mason tended to provide the vegetables for their sustenance and the well which provided water for the house and surrounds, the cattle had been bought to the house paddock to wean off the calves, a job Marie with the help of Mollie and Mason was going to have to do herself within the next day or two. The fifteen cattle and ten calves were their main asset.

The house was a solid cob building which her Father had built so many years ago and she could recall the neighbours helping and the celebrations the night it was finished and the family had finally moved into after living in the wagon and tents for so long.

Their two dogs were still tied near their kennels beside the Barn, that had stood since the farm was first settled after the 'Trek,' and lay in its shade.

It was mid morning when she saw the dust rising in the distance and in due course several wagons and soldiers rode into the yard.

The procession was led by a Brigadier, a Sergeant with several Corporals and a number of Infantry,with five supporting wagons, two of which held a mix of furniture and obviously other Mothers and children and the others laden with a mixture of vegetables, meat, tools and other accoutrements ; the Brigadier dismounted and walked towards Marie and the servants and children gathered at the stoep .

'Good morning Madam, is your husband not here?' 'May I ask where he is as I should like to talk to him' 'You have received notice of the 'Oath of Allegiance' you are both required to sign and I have it with me, do we wait for your Husband ?'

'My Husband is away, however , I speak for both of us, we do not intend to sign the 'Oath of Allegiance' Marie replied.

'I wish you had decided otherwise but it is your decision and you must accept the consequences, I advise you as follows:' he responded and began reading from a prompt obviously prepared for such events

I inform you that your husband , yourself and your children are to be evacuated and will be concentrated into a regional camp . This is for your own safety . Take only what you can carry . No servants and no livestock' 'I note your husband is away , I advise that if he is with the rebels , as I suspect , such protection is withdrawn and he is regarded as an enemy of the British forces and will be treated as such.'

'You have one hour to prepare, I advise you not to waste any of that time'

'Sergeant begin'

The soldiers formed into squads under their Corporals, one squad which included the New Zealanders, James and Bill was despatched to the garden and began pulling all the vegetables and loading onto a wagon. They were spreading salt over the cleared areas as they were completed 'Christ Bill I never thought we would come to a war and end up as vandals, if you were in New Zealand flogging vegetables you could go before the beak' James said recollecting his own experience. 'what a bastard of a fucking job!'

A second squad had taken the dogs behind the sheds and next thing there were the retorts of rifles and all barking stopped, that squad then began to herd the stock to the track and to drove them away.

When James' squad had completed the destruction of the garden they were instructed to fell all the fruit trees and fire the outbuildings.

In the meantime another squad had slaughtered the pigs and chickens and were disembowelling and drawing them before loading to another wagon; as they were completed the offal, feathers, heads and guts were being thrown down the well ' that will stop any Boers that think they might get a drink here' one of the squad laughed.

In the interim Marie had come out of the house with a bible and books for the children and old lithographs from the house plus some food in a hamper and clothes in a battered suitcase. Her and the children were marched to one of the wagons and with some difficulty were accommodated on the back amongst heaps of salvaged furniture and household effects randomly thrown over the wagon.

'The Kaffirs can walk with the others' said the Brigadier 'it's not far anyway, lead off Sergeant' and the assembled wagons began to turn and start travelling back in the direction from whence they had come.

When the convoy was about half a kilometre from the farm Marie was looking back at her home, when suddenly there was an explosion and she saw one of the Corporals rise from where he had sheltered behind the well foundations and from where he had obviously set off a charge. The house had burst at the walls and the thatched roof began to blaze as it drifted through the air, together with any flammable materials that had been left, and the cob walls were being strewn in a rough circle about where the house had stood.

Johannes and Marriette began to cry and Marie was having difficulty hiding her emotions, a mixture of sadness and hate 'I do hope we have made the right decision' she wondered as they trekked away from her life to date and tried to console and hush the weeping children.

It was early afternoon when they arrived at the rail siding, there was a proliferation of troops and wagons, horses, mules and oxen, some other livestock and produce and other materials from a number of farms around the siding area.

The black slaves stood remote from the Boer wives and children

Marie sighted and waved to Mason and Millie who were standing near the rear of the train .

'Stay away from them, there will be no fraternising between you and the Kaffirs', a number of soldiers began to threaten with their rifles and move the women and children back .

Marie and a host of others trudged towards waiting stock trucks 'surely do not tell me we are to travel in those' she thought 'surely the Englishers will have some measure of decency'

'Get into the wagons' was the order and Marie passed up Mariette to waiting arms and assisted Johannes into the first stock wagon and climbed herself, assisted by other arms .

Beyond them the blacks were being loaded into similar stock wagons near the rear of the train.

The wagon had been lined between the planked sides of the stock wagon and it was impossible to see out, some light and air came from the spaces in the roof planking and the floor which was uncovered and stank of excreta, piss and human and animal smells. In the far corner was a bucket and the rest of the wagon was bare of any other fittings.

'Find yourself a space and sit down, no noise, we leave as soon as the train is loaded, you will be fed and watered later, a bucket is provided if you need to relieve yourselves' one of the Soldiers called out.

Marie and the children sat near the side of the wagon as it began to fill, until there were nearly seventy women and children inside, when the sliding doors were pulled to and they sat in the semi darkness with the others. The wagon was filled with the noise of sobbing children and Mothers trying to calm them while resisting the urge to break down and cry with them 'hush' Marie tried to calm the children, 'it will soon be over and we will have our new place to live until we are reunited with your Father one day – be strong'

Throughout the rest of the afternoon women and children were unable to control themselves any longer and were forced to use the bucket for their ablutions, there was no water to wash and after finishing the bucket was upended and tipped down a hole through the floor onto the tracks below.

There was such a queue at times that several were unable to wait their turn and simply squatted near to the end of the wagon near the bucket and the floor began to get more emissions of bodily waste over it; the stench was becoming unbearable and everyone began to press towards the other end of the wagon to escape the mess and the smell.

It was not until late that afternoon that the train began to pull out from the siding, the wagon was now extremely hot and with no water and the conditions worsening all the time, all the children and some of the Mothers were beginning to flag.

That evening they pulled to a halt and the sliding doors were opened ' thank God'said Marie we can now get some fresh air, instead soldiers threw in a store of pannikins and placed a large container of water and another of sou , with vegetables and pieces of meat, at the doors which were then pulled to and relocked from the outside.

There was an instant rush and water was being spilt as Mothers were pushing in trying to ensure they got their share of the water and then the soup, all in the half dark of the evening made worse by the enclosed sides of the wagon.

Marie finally got water for the children and managed to get one pannikin of soup before it was all gone, despite frantic cries to the soldiers outside, no more water or soup was supplied, just an instruction 'you will have to learn how to share, we have no more for you'

Minutes later and the train rolled on again, however as the night lengthened, the cold descended to the dark interior of the wagon, everyone was forced to huddle together trying desperately to gain some warmth from one another, and there were early arguments and a few fisticuffs and battles until they all came to understand they had to compromise and help each other or some of them, especially the older Mothers and younger children, may not survive the night as the temperature plunged.

Next morning at about 6:00 the train again drew to a halt on a siding and sometime later the ritual of water and soup was repeated and after a brief period the train again began to roll forward. In spite of their protestations none of the children or adults had been allowed to leave the wagon for fresh air or to receive any attention.

Mariette and some of the other children were beginning to tremble, some were very pale , and closing their eyes, their foreheads were hot to the touch and Marie and the other Mothers were trying her best to keep them awake until they stopped again and they could get some assistance, other women were lending assistance, advice and comfort to Marie and the others 'they must be alright, it can't be long now before we reach our destination and they can get a doctor' they said however, a number of them kept slipping in and out of consciousness.

In the afternoon Mariette closed her eyes for the last time, Marie and the others were unable to rouse her until finally one of them said 'she has no pulse, I am sorry she has gone to the Lord' Marie was devastated, they had only left their home yesterday, fit and healthy and already her Daughter had succumbed to the conditions, how much more would she endure before they reached the camp.

The train stopped on a siding again that evening by which time two other young children had passed away, this time when the doors opened the women began to scream at the soldiers to look after the children and demanded to see the leading Officer and a doctor.

The Brigadier came to the door of the carriage 'it is obvious that several of your children have not been cared for properly and there have been a number of children die which is most distressing to my troops, they are preparing a communal grave and we will have a service and internment shortly, please pass out any children that have passed away, their Mothers and family may accompany them, everyone else is to stay in the wagons, we will feed you after that, no doctor is available until we reach the camp, you must take better care of your charges'

Marie, passed the still form of Mariette to a waiting soldier ' God keep the little one' he muttered, Marie and Johannes got down from the carriage and she recovered her daughter, along the length of the wagons there were other Mothers and children lining up, about twenty five in all with near ten dead children, 'how many more will there be unless we get to the camps soon' Marie thought .

The communal grave had been dug some distance from the tracks ' we have no spare wood for coffins but will wrap the bodies in canvas shrouds, you have 10 minutes to say your goodbye and then the service will begin' said the Brigadier.

The weeping and sobbing Mothers and siblings sat beside their loved ones as they were placed in the shrouds, praying silently or out loud, as they were passed down to soldiers standing in the grave who laid them alongside one another.

The Officers and Soldiers stood to attention, with rifles at the slope, as the Padre intoned 'Lord receive these children victims of a cruel war and a lack of care, suffer them to come unto you for redemption and a realisation of the true Christian faith, bless them all as we who are left pray *Our Father whom art in heaven , hallowed be thy name , thy kingdom come, it will be done on earth as it is in Heaven , and give us this day our daily bread , and forgive our trespass as we forgive those who trespass against us , and deliver us from evil , for thine is the power and the glory , Amen'*

'Thank you Gentlemen, you can now fill in the graves and erect a marker with the names of those interred' ' the rest of you internees reboard the wagons and we will shortly have an evening meal and water, albeit a bit belated , then carry on, I expect to reach the Camp at about 7:00 am tomorrow and he wheeled and returned to his carriage.

That night was again cold and in the morning another 4 children had perished, it was a sad and chastened group who exited the wagons as the train pulled up to the concentration camp .

'All out, fall into lines and await your registration and instructions.'

The women and children assembled outside the gates to the Camp. It stretched in the distance in both directions, surrounded by high wire fences and with barbed wire entanglements both sides of the gate, it was a mass of tents with several large buildings, at the distant corners were elevated observation posts with two guards, and a machine gun, watching the people congregating outside the tents and in front of the wagons of the train.

The camp was situated with a small river and some trees along one boundary but on the other three sides, and beyond the watercourse, stretched across a featureless landscape to distant mountains.

'What are you doing with our servants' Marie asked one of the soldiers. The train is taking them to their own camp was the muttered reply ' no talking' called out one of the Sergeants 'any fraternising with the enemy and you will be on a charge', he added.

'Pay attention, I am the Commandant of this camp provided for your protection, those people with deceased or ill children or relatives are to be taken to a place of burial which has been provided, and they will be placed with the other victims of this war and this camp, to date'

'The rest of you will check in to the Officers recording your details, you will be allocated space in a tent, you will find your way there you are too late now for Breakfast so you will have to wait for the evening meal; I advise that you are not to make contact with any of the soldiers, speak only when you are spoken to, do not attempt escape, there is nowhere for you to go and when we catch you, as we will, you will be brought back to camp and punished severely or shot dependent on the circumstance of your escape' with that the Commandant began to walk away to one of the buildings nearby.

Marie and the others lined up and began making their way towards the several tables where an Officer sat at each table with a scribe recording details and issuing instructions.

'Names' was the curt direction.

'Marie van Bruin and my son Johannes van Bruin' she said .

'Do you have any other children not with you' she was asked . Marie nodded her head No as tears rolled down her cheeks, she was issued with two pannikins .

'Control yourself Madam' the Officer said 'row 12 tent 107, you will find all you need there'

Marie and Johannes trudged after the some of the others until she located row 12 and they began a long walk past assembled tents to number 107 marked with a stamped number on the fly .

They entered the tent to see two other women inside lying on two of the four stretcher beds, they were dishevelled and gaunt with open staring eyes .

'Well look what the cats dragged in' one of them said 'a pity the young one is a bit too young but we have to make do, grab a bed I am Aletta and this other lady is Brunelda, forgive us if we don't get up but we are resting to receive some beauty time, make yourselves at home, spread out and enjoy the British hospitality and good luck to you, you will need it'

Besides the stretchers there was a small dresser with two drawers and a bucket beside it the rest of the tent was sparse with a few clothes strewn on the baked clay floor, the flap of the tent was open but it was still stifling hot inside the tent 'sorry about the heat, we haven't got any slaves to wave fans for us and its even hotter outside' said Aletta , obviously the dominant person in the tent 'rest up, dinner isn't for a couple of hours yet, if you can call it that, we are on half rations apparently as the fucking Brits don't have enough food for us and more people are coming in every day, God knows they can't give us any less half of us are dying of starvation now' she added.

'Please don't speak like that in front of my son' said Marie ; he has been well brought up and not used to such language, I don't believe all you say, I thought the British are a civilised race although after our train trip I wonder, however, I have been told there are doctors and a hospital here so it can't be all bad'

'Well listen to Mrs High and Mighty, you will soon come down a peg or two, I hope you know how to spread your legs or you might not get enough to live on here with the meagre rations, your Son is going to grow up mighty fast if he's going to survive. You have got a lot to learn about your fucking civilised Brits and I hope you don't end up in their one way Hospitals is all I can say' and Aletta lay back and ignored them any further.

After an afternoon where Marie and Johannes attempted to sleep, but interrupted by various whistles about every two hours, a siren sounded and they followed the rest of the prisoners towards a station set up to issue the evening meal. 'what is that constant whistling for?' Marie asked one of the women 'that's another death in the camp' was the response.

It was a soup of various vegetables with a modicum of some sort of meat floating in it, they received a half a pannikin each and a lump of dry bread 'water is available after your meal' they were advised, remember to bring back your pannikin .

Where are the lavatories Marie asked a woman next to her 'they are those trenches over there' was the response .

Marie looked and gasped, they were open trenches with a timber plank each side braced above the ground, they had a canvas stretched along the front to give some semblance of privacy although one was going to have to walk past all the occupied areas to find a space

'What about children' she asked.

'I suggest you hold tightly to them' was the retort 'else they would surely drown or worse if they fell in'

After their Tea, Marie pulled their stretcher out to the front of the tent and her and Johannes sat in the evening light, shortly some other Mothers and children made their way out and the children began to play a game with an old sock rolled up as a ball and two sticks, one each end as makeshift goals. Marie was still hungry but assumed the rations must be enough for them to survive 'maybe I can lose some weight for Wilhelm' she thought.

The days dragged on, without anything to do she tried to keep Johannes occupied with stories about their land and life to date. How she had been with her parents on the great trek to their homelands \.

Tales of the long battles with the Zulus who numbered in the tens of thousands when they attacked the wagon trains and how desperately they had fought and finally the attacks had stopped after they had united with the British against the common enemy.

Tales of the British at Rourkes Drift and of the Boers own survival

About his Father Wilhelm and his principled stand for freedom for the Boers again and reminding him that he was to be strong for his Father and look after her and pray for his return at the end of the war.

She talked of the faithful servants Mason and Millie who had both helped raise the children and teach them a little of their ways.

And finally she talked of the children she had lost through the years and how happy her and Wilhelm had been when they finally had raised the two of them Johannes and Mariette. Of her heartache with Mariettes passing away.

Every day for the next several weeks she talks and talks but every day she realizes both of them getting weaker and weaker.

There are the constant whistles throughout every day as more and more children and women are dying and being taken to the common burial ground behind the camp.

The words of Aletta and Brunelda have been prophetic and although many women and children go to the hospital they are either sent away again to die for lack of medicines or they are dying in the hospital.

The half rations are beginning to have an effect and are barely sufficient to survive, in fact many are not and succumbing not a death by starvation, others are resorting to clandestine meetings at night by the 'hole in the fence' and receive an apple or slice of bread to supplement the meagre existence and try to stay alive.

'I will not lower myself and shame my husband by doing that, no matter what' Marie thinks to herself in spite of the constant jeers from the other two in the tent 'it's the only way you will get some semblance of food in this place' they admonish.

Marie is near collapse with hunger and exhaustion and Wilhelm is failing when one day one of the soldiers speaks to her outside the tent 'goodness me' he begins 'you were on a farm we sacked some weeks ago how are you faring?' he asks

After he has offered to help her that night Marie agrees to meet him after he has promised he only wants to help her.

Aletta and Brunelda do not know the latter reason for her going but agree to look after Wilhelm and laugh as they think she has finally relented and decided to join the others for a bit of fun and she leaves at 8:00 to meet the young man who had called himself Bill.

He gives her a slice of bread he had salvaged from his meal and promises to get her some more in a couple of days and for a while they lay side by side on the river bank and he tells about his life in New Zealand, his sister Millicent and his disillusionment with the war, about the stars in the sky and describes the Southern Cross which she had known as the 'kite' from her childhood and for a brief time she believes she may come through this experience although deep down she is entering a deep depression.

Back at the tent later that night she is pestered by the other two women 'well how did it go , what was it like etc' although Marie will not respond

She feeds the slice of bread, except for one small bite for herself to Wilhelm who is only able to moan in answer to her concerns about 'how are you little one?' and a short time later he is violently ill vomiting up the food he had just eaten and beginning to shake violently, she picked him up and ran to the hospital to be told he had Malaria, that there was no quinine available as it was all required for the troops but she had better leave him there that night and return in the morning.

It was a saddened Marie who trudged back to the tent for once the others were reserved and contrite wishing her well for the wee chap.

In the morning she is told ' your son passed away in the night, he did not suffer, you may spend ten minutes and say goodbye'

A short time later he is buried with a number of other children in a shared canvas shroud and her and other Mothers attend a short graveside service where the British Padre intones a service and then walks away. There is no time to grieve over the graves before they are sent back to their tents.

Marie lies forlorn on her bed after Aletta and Brunelda have expressed their condolences she thinks 'last night I foolishly thought things could get better' and in her rundown state her grief begins to overwhelm her 'it is never going to improve, I have lost both my children and I don't even know if Wilhelm is still alive' she thinks. The other two have left the tent to walk around the camp and leave her to her sorrows.

Suddenly she decides 'I have had all I can take' she tears a strip from her sole blanket and twists it into a semblance of a rope and ties it to the top of the ridge pole of the tent making sure it is held by the ferrule of the pole where it enters the top of the canvas, she tips up the bucket from the corner of the tent and stands on it while tying the rope as taut as she can around her neck and kicks the bucket away.

For several minutes she struggles as slowly she is being strangled to death, her body acting in one final frenzy against and resisting the final moments as she swings against the tent pole trying vainly to seek a foothold until finally her body succumbs and she hangs lifeless.

Chapter 14 : Some of the Aftermath

The War is over

May 1902

The second Boer war is over at last, the church bells in England chime and throughout the Empire the populace is heartened by the resolution and strength of the British Empire and its ability to control the vast territories it administers, and a proof that rebellion will not win out.

One wonders whether if Gold and Diamonds had not been discovered, if the Afrikaners had simply bowed to pressure and given the franchise to the 'uitlanders' who had ventured into the Orange Free State and Transvaal what would have been the end outcome because this was quoted as one of the reasons for the conflict, although there were other tangled reasons which no one could really recall. Maybe the Boers would have continued to be farmers and the miners and adventurers to be just that but with a voice in the administration of the two states: somebody had said at the end of it all *'maybe Kruger should have just given them the vote but made sure he counted them!'*

There have been some strange descriptions of tactics and a new type of total war which will set the tone for future conflicts. Lord Roberts when beginning the 'Scorched Earth Policy' had said 'it is absolutely essential to force the people to submit and it is now clear that this can only be done by severe measure. You must have no mercy and what you cannot bring away you must destroy, however to his small credit he did allow that those Boers who alleged allegiance to the British were able to stay on their farms, a circumstance which only lasted for a few weeks before total destruction and incarceration began.

Kitchener has described it as 'the last Gentlemans war' although many would disagree with his definition and he has been the driving force which intensified the use of the camps as a way to force surrender, a process which has taken nearly another two years post the annexation of the Orange Free State and Transvaal when Lord Roberts has left satisfied with his efforts 'job done, and war effectively over!'

For the first time in history more non combatants than combatants have died in a war and most of them have been children under the age of sixteen.

At the commencement of the 'scorched earth policy' those Boers that had sworn allegiance were spared the loss of their farms, livestock, crops and lifestyle but in the second part of the offensive when the rebel Boers were continuing to wreak havoc with their Guerilla raids and lightning fast attacks these latter properties were destroyed as well. In the end over 30,000 farms and several small towns and villages have been sacked and destroyed not including the hundreds of Native Kraals similarly included. The Black natives concentration camps were established because Kitchener wanted to make sure that no aid was given to the Boers (a remarkable thought when many of them were slaves) and to give a resource of labourers to build blockhouses, barbed wire fences and work the Gold and Diamond mines as the security of these locations was ensured.

Over 110,000 White women, children and elderly have been incarcerated in 42 concentration camps and although records are sparse in this latter regard a large number of Blacks have been interred in their own British concentration camps. 26,300 have died in the White camps, of which 22,000 are children, and about 14,500 in the Black camps about two thirds children, the figures for the Blacks are of a lesser percentage than for the white camps, a result of releasing many of the Blacks throughout the latter stages of the conflict to work for the British and the lower concentrations and reduced disease. Emily Hobhouse and the later government inspectors did not view or comment on conditions in the Black camps and there are very little records in existence. The war has seen the first use of concentration camps to depopulate entire regions and oppress a civilian population although towards the end of the conflict and now that the civilian authorities are managing the camps Kitchener has ordered that many of the women and children are simply abandoned among the ruins of their farms so that they are a burden on their menfolk and do not require any action to transport them by the army. There are no records of how many more have perished under these circumstances.

After Emily Hobhouse had made her trip and described the terrible conditions in the Concentration camps to a doubting public and Press, subsequently verified by the Governments own Millicent Fawcett and the growing unrest post this disclosure by the public and Parliament the civilian authorities took over the administration of the camps from the Army and the mortality rate plunged as the conditions markedly improved, however at the end of the conflict most of the prisoners had no home to return to and were forced to remain in the camp environment and were looked after by the authorities.

Readers Note: Emily Hobhouse was the only non South African to ever have a memorial erected in that country and her Obelisk is at the site of the first Concentration camp near Bloemfontein and is now the Anglo/ Boer Museum

The World could not fail to be impressed with the 'brave OR foolhardy?' defence of their principles by a force in total throughout the war of less than 45,000 Boers against the greatest military power in the world with over 450,000 Empire troops engaged throughout the course of the conflict supported by a total blockade of the coastline by the Royal Navy with a huge fleet of ships which ensured the provision of arms and munitions from countries sympathetic to the Boer cause for example German East Africa was extremely limited. Although the Boers enjoyed considerable early success with their established forces and field pieces and laid siege to places like Ladysmith and Mafeking they were never realistically going to be able to resist the immense forces thrown against them. At Spionkop for example the Boers had defeated a hugely superior British force with 1683 British killed for the loss of 198 Boers and Britain was never going to 'take that lying down' and these types of frontal battles and sieges were going to be a thing of the past as the Boers were forced to resort to Guerilla war an arena in which they excelled with their superior horsemanship, marksmanship and knowledge of the country and environment and enjoying considerable success which only began to slow as the Colonial troops, more suited to and experienced in this environment, equalled and sometimes bettered the Boer in their own backyard supported by the slow erosion of resources as the conflict continued.

In common with most wars a sense of Patriotism and duty calls young men from far and wide to defend whatever the 'cause of the day' is and in the Victorian age these allegiances and love of the Queen and Empire were ingrained into society and very strong and thus bought many Colonial forces to a venue where they could prove 'their mettle and strength and bring a sense of Nationhood to the young countries of Canada, New Zealand, Australia and hopefully a recognition and self governance in respect of India who has sent significant numbers to the 'cause'; actually a 'lost cause' as Indian independence is still near 50 years away in spite of their contribution to this and future conflicts.

It is a time for White men and exampled by the utterance of Seddon Prime Minister of New Zealand agitating to enter the conflict when he said *'our race could be, and should be the dominant race of the world'* a view widely held at that time and even propagated to the populace by the Churches of the time and the Politicians of White nations around the World.

A young Winston Churchill has come to an increased prominence in England, in 1899 he was a correspondent for the 'London Morning Post' and was actually being paid more than Rudyard Kipling and Arthur Conan Doyle who were also reporters in Africa at the time, Winston was 24 years of age when war broke out, he promptly became a war correspondent and almost immediately had set off by train to South Africa. The train was delayed by a force of Boers who had placed rocks on the track and caused a derailment and they were jubilant indeed when they discovered one of their captives was Winston Churchill who was already a famous personality. He was incarcerated in a jail in Pretoria and made a daring escape by vaulting a fence and fleeing via a neighbouring property and thence he made his way finally exhausted to a farmhouse which luckily was occupied by an English family and he hid in an abandoned mine for a number of days before continuing his escape until finally safe in Mozambique.

During his escape a reward of 25 pounds had been offered for his capture 'Dead or Alive' and after being feted throughout England he returned, riding a horse in the advance into Pretoria as it fell to Empire forces, releasing the prisoners from the jail where he had been imprisoned and actually took part in at least one battle *'Spion Kop' a famous war battle scene (and celebrated in New Zealand's Tararua mountain range where one of the peaks bears that name.)*

He had written a letter which he had left with his captor Hendrick Spaarwater who he had been well treated by, which said *'The bearer Mr H.G. Spaarwater has been very kind to me and the British Officers captured in the Escort Armoured Train. I shall be personally grateful to anyone who may be able to do him any service should he himself be taken prisoner – Winston S. Churchill'* Churchill later cited this letter in a book he wrote called *'London to Ladysmith via Pretoria'* and it is still in existence and offered for sale in 2020 for $85,000

Winstons bravery was recognised when post the war he entered Parliament in England as a very popular candidate and MP and his actions were lauded and quoted often as a hugely popular example of the British Bulldog strength of character.

At the end of the day about 22,000 British soldiers have died but about 13,000 of them from disease, it is thought that somewhat less than this number of Boers have been killed and of the Colonial forces about 1000 have been killed. Contrast this with about 40,000 deaths in the concentration camps nearly 65% of which were children and these latter figures are quite horrific.

A number of strange things had occurred; in 1900 France and Russia have asked Kaiser Wilhelm II to form an alliance and attack Britain while they are busy with the Boers. Although Germany has no love for Britain it declines the invitation and Wilhelm II tells

Queen Victoria, his Grandmother (*Wilhelms mother was Victoria the oldest daughter of Queen Victoria of Britain*)

Queen Victoria had knitted 8 scarves to be awarded for acts of bravery and 4 were to be for the Colonial troops specifically. They were Khaki and initialled VRI and were to be awarded 4 to British troops and 4 to Colonial troops for "best all round man" they were duly given out I each to an Australian, a new Zealander, a Canadian and the last intended for a member of the South African Empire forces actually given to an American who had been part of a contingent who delivered mules from America to the British and had stayed on for 'a bit of a scrap'.

Readers Note: 2 of the Colonials were actually recommended for a Victoria Cross but given a scarf instead , all of the scarves are still in existence in military museums.

After the trial and execution of 'Breaker Morant' by a British military court *(mysteriously most of the transcript of the trial is lost)* Australia reconsiders its position and in future conflicts it will insist its troops have their own command and never again will an Australian soldier be condemned and executed by the British army a policy sadly not implemented by the other colonials!

The Australians have proved themselves on the battle fields and have been feared by the Boer and admired by many other troops along with the new Zealanders they have been recognized as proud allies to the Empire cause.

After the British army had recruited troops from the lower classes of society and specifically in London and discovered the poor physical condition of the men (where 7 out of every 9 have proved unfit for service), and generally the population, especially the poor of the slums, social reforms were introduced throughout England in the form of destruction of the infested slums, education and fitness with Baden- Powell introducing the 'Scouts' movement to improve the sporting prowess and fitness of young men, later the introduction of 'Cubs' or young Scouts with trainers named after the characters in Kiplings 'The Jungle Book', plus a host of general reforms, improved sanitation with reticulated sewer systems, housing, washhouses and communal facilities and other major social reforms including education; these all echoed similar social improvements that Germany in particular had implemented some years previously and for similar reasons.

The Canadians had led the first British success against the Boers at Paardeberg and had sent 40 teachers post the war to teach the children and help rebuild the country. Many Canadians were disillusioned with the British efforts during the conflict and were scornfull of many of the practices and especially the Concentration Camps leading to a loosening of the ties to England. A Canadian Surgeon John McCrae who had been in the Boer war would later serve in the First World War and pen the famous words to *'In Flanders Fields'*

As for the defeated Boers well? after the war the two republics, Orange Free State and Transvaal are given self government including the use of Afrikaans in Schools, Courts and government departments. The British have paid millions of pounds in compensation for war damage and no decision has been made in respect of Black enfranchisement so once again one could surmise they have been 'screwed' and received no recognition or reward for their contribution to the Empire cause; similarly India will have to wait about another 50 years for its independence. *It is of interest that a young Indian activist has served as a volunteer stretcher bearer in the Indian forces seeking that recognition and independence for his country; his name was Mahatma Ghandi.*

In short not much different to any other war at the end of the day, and hard to decide who won or lost?

And what of our characters ?

From the Transvaal, Wilhelm, Marie and their two children are all dead, the end of the whole family when Wilhelm was killed, actually 4 days after the end of the war !

Louis is left alone, his farm is destroyed and he has decided that there is a future in becoming a hunting guide, many of the British gentry are desirous of the thrill of the hunt and trophies to bedeck their mansions and halls and are prepared to pay good money for the opportunity and services provided and Louis cannot afford a conscience against his previous enemy and decides if someone is going to make money out of this it may as well be him. If he loses a few clients so be it as long as they have paid up front first, some of this hunting isn't going to be anything like chasing Foxes on horseback!

James Merritt with his dreams of a new life for himself and Mary in South Africa is also dead a victim on the same date and place as Wilhelm, two people from different societies and half a world apart from their birthplaces in a macabre twist of fate and after the official end of hostilities.

Our two Australians David and John have survived the conflict had plenty of fun along the way and have a fortune in gold waiting for them as their reward, all they have to do is get it. As volunteers in the Bushveldt Carbineers as soon as hostilities have ended they are out of it with a pocket full of pay from a grateful British Government and still in South Africa ready to recover the gold bullion as soon as possible and begin the life of luxury they reckon they deserve !

And finally Bill the New Zealander has been given his discharge from the army and advised his parents he intends to stay on in South Africa for a while, to have a good look at some of the country again and to obtain some trophy animals on hunting safaris, to have them mounted and sent back to New Zealand for the family home before he returns to the farm and his birthright . His Pater has send him a generous amount of funds to pursue his aspirations and his Mater and Sister Millicent sent him their best wishes and are looking forward to his return.

Our two Canadians are off to explore the area towards and the city of Wanderfontein before they return home and Richard begins married life

Chapter 15 : After the War

Louis the hunting guide and Bill Gibson his client

Pretoria Transvaal June 1902

Louis had received compensation from the interim government and had some residual funds of own but barely enough to set up his recreational game hunting business.

He spent each night outside the bars and shantys waiting until a sole drinker exited to relieve himself in the adjacent alleys where he would give them a stiff rabbit punch to the back of the neck, several times he wondered if he had been a bit too rough but he determined that he was only going to administer revenge to outsiders, that is to say English or their allies in the last war so his conscience was not worried when a few of them looked like they may never rise again. Strangely they also seemed to be the most flush with funds so as he rapidly emptied their pockets and purses his funds were accumulating nicely until after perhaps a month, and in spite of numerous warnings to patrons to use the 'in house' facilities instead of the normally stinking and overflowing long drop dunnies most establishments had at the rear of their bars, Louis had sufficient funds to embark on his business.

Horses were easy to procure, almost all of the horses imported from the United States of America and the mounts bought to South Africa by the Colonial forces and most of the English mounts had either been slaughtered to feed the population in the old camps which were near full of people who had found they had nowhere to go after the conflict or they had been set free to wander and graze where they could and it was a simple task to collect a team of good looking and sound mounts, wagons were also not difficult to locate as they had been abandoned in their hundreds and a couple of the best were selected and outfitted for hunting.

Louis had purchased an arsenal of rifles and ammunition but had given preference to the Mauser arms with which he had fought his war and used as a young man, although he had a variety of other rifles, shotguns for big game and wild fowl and was well equipped.

He had purchased cases of ammunition and other weapons, knives, ropes, pulleys, tack for the horses and grain and provisions, large quantities of salt for preserving hides until they could be tanned, ropes, tents and arranged a taxidermist, had employed several Blacks, reoutfitted himself in a set of clean and serviceable clothes and was frequenting the local watering holes and respectable saloons seeking a client or clients, in expectation of interest he had printed a few posters which showed a stylised Louis standing proudly atop a dead Lion accompanied by his name 'Louis Badenhorst – Professional Big Game Hunter and Guide', he had indicated to the barmen and staff who he was with the promise of a cash bonus if they could line him up with a client .

It was only a few nights later that as he entered one of the bars the barman directed him to a table of English officers with the message 'one of those wants to go hunting' Louis duly gave him a shilling with his thanks.

Louis approached the table and enquired 'good evening, I am Louis Badenhorst, I understand one of you wants to go on a hunting trip

'I say have you had much experience in this sort of thing' one of the English Colonels addressed him as his fellow officers looked on 'I don't want anyone who might cut and run, how much experience have you had, the word of a barman doesn't give me any idea, if I am after a Lion I don't want someone in a blue funk who will let me down ?'

Louis drew to his full height dwarfing the Englishmen 'listen here you toffee nosed bastard, I have lived here all my life and I shot and killed my first Lion when I was 9 years old in 1885 and I know the secrets of hunting, can you bloody keep up your end of it ?'

'I will not be spoken to in that manner you uncouth savage, my family has hunted since before you were born, be off and come back if you can learn some manners or don't bother annoying me again' as his friends looked on as though they were ready to rise in defence of their friend.

Louis face reddened and he glared at the Colonel 'talk to me like that ever again and I will thrash you within an inch of your life' he was having great difficulty in holding back his temper and resisting the urge to start right that moment, instead he turned on his heel and stormed out.

'I am going to have to eat humble pie and approach these wallahs a bit more respectfully or I am not going to get any work' he thought to himself as he stormed out 'my first foray into being a guide hasn't worked out too well'

It was a more contrite and respectful Louis that found himself the next day meeting up with a New Zealander who had been asking for a hunting guide.

'Shake hands' said Bill looking Louis in the eye 'my name is Bill and I am from New Zealand, I want some trophies to send back home, that barman over there told you are the best hunter in South Africa, and so did a couple of those fellows over there, mates of yours are they, sit down and lets have a beer and talk about it'

Louis thought to himself 'what a good barman! I only met him yesterday' this looks like a more likely character to take hunting anyway. He spoke 'I don't know those people over there but anyway I am intending to charge a pound a day for myself and I have ten Blacks who will be with us who are three shillings a day each, I will supply everything – what do want to hunt?'

'That sounds all right to me, I want some trophies to take back home so they would have to be mounted, we have plenty of Deer and Pigs trophies at home so what do you suggest, I'm willing to learn from you'

Louis was heartened by this 'this fellow seems like he might be alright' he thought and said 'first of all we will have to go East towards the mountains to get into the open veldt so that will take a few days travel, but we can travel light if you are okay with that and some of the 'boys' can bring up the wagons and supplies each night and you might get a chance on the way, you can take your pick but we always had a few Zebra skins which are pretty distinctive if you want a few of them, there are Gemsbok (I think you call them Oryx) and if you can get a good female they have real nice long straight horns, if you want twisting horns you can have an Impala, there's Wildebeest if you want a set of real big horns and then there are

Cheetah, Lions, Springbok, Elephants and Rhino you take your pick really depends how many and what you want?'

'Have you done any hunting before Bill' he asked

I have shot a few animals while in South Africa when on scouting duties for the army and we supplemented our meals with a bit of game from time to time, not really sport we just chased them down with horses and men until we could fire a few shots and lower some, pretty indiscriminate as we were only after some meat. A lot of the game disappeared before we got there with all the racket an army makes !'

'We have Pigs and Deer in New Zealand as game animals and I have hunted both of them, Deer require a permit so generally only one a year but I do go and practice a bit of stalking and there are plenty of Pigs which we chase with dogs and stick with a knife unless they are real big Boars when we might have to shoot them, I have seen lots of game here mostly from a distance except as I said before'

'I don't want to try taking an Elephant or even its foot and a Rhino is a bit big too but I thought one each of the horned animals mounted would look good when I get home and you are right maybe a few nice skins, no problem to get them mounted or tanned?'

'No I have a taxidermist arranged, his costs will be extra but Gemsbok and Wildebeest he told me are about two and four pounds each respectively including a shield so that will give you some idea, sound alright?' was Louis' response.

'Right that's settled, I'm ready whenever you are, I have a bit of kit and a horse and tack of my own anyway when do we go?' Bill said

'Give me a day to complete the supplies and outfit us and get the 'boys' together and we will set off, we will be going east towards Barberton then heading South before we get there, we will be hunting the swamps, gullies and scrub areas bordering the veldt, where are you staying? I will meet you outside at 5:00 am the day after tomorrow and we are off, I will want fifty pound up front before we go'

'Good stuff, I'll bring the money with me and have another beer on the strength of it' Bill stood and raised to shake hands on the deal. 'look forward to having a few good times out there'

'I don't know why you came half way round the world to destroy our farms and way of life, to murder our women and children and kill and maim some of my friends, this is a business and I will give you a good hunt but we are never going to be friends so you had better realize that before we start, I shake hands because we have an agreement and that's all' 'we will get on all right just don't expect me to like you or any of your type' Louis snorted 'I can't forget just like that although you might think it was all just bloody good fun'

'Listen mate, I want to forget it all too, I was disillusioned with the war for a while and I've been waiting a long time for it to over, I have lost my best mate as well so it wasn't all one sided, if you lot hadn't been so bloody pig headed it would have been finished a couple of years ago I don't have to be friends with you to enjoy the hunting experience so take the chip off your shoulder, we have to get along and if that doesn't suit you the deals off!'

Louis thought 'hell I am on the verge of losing my second hire in two days 'alright, sorry I flew off the handle a bit, you are right we have to get on together' and Louis extended his hand 'can we still have that beer?'

Pretoria 2nd June 1902

Dear Mater , Pater and Millicent,

I have some tragic news for you, you will recall my friend James Merritt who enlisted the same day as me and has been my companion throughout the war.

James was tragically killed 4 days after the end of hostilities when we were on patrol seeking Boers to take to our HQ post surrender when he was shot by a Boer sniper , one would imagine who was not aware the war was over.

I was terribly cut up about it and still am, his fiancee Mary was to have come out to be married and I was to be Best Man for them, such is war I suppose but it seems awfully unfair somehow.

So be it and I just have to carry one without his companionship.

Well I am about to set off on a safari , the local name for a hunting expedition.

I have engaged a Boer as a guide, he has lost his family farm in the war so has turned his hand to hunting

I am led to believe he is very good at his job and has a reputation known far and wide among the local population as he was abandoned by his Father in the middle of the plains when he was 9 years old with a couple of black servants only about 13 years old and he managed to get them back to the farm with an animal he had killed plus he had shot a Lion and protected them.

Quite a story but he seems a pretty moody sort of a chap which I can understand a bit, all things considered, so lets hope he thaws out a bit or it will be a long journey.

I expect it will take about a couple of weeks or so to get the trophies I want and I will then arrange to come home

I had no trouble with a discharge from the army as several chaps have decided to stay on in South Africa , there certainly seem to be some good opportunities for them with the armed constabulary and with a pay rate about 4 times what they were receiving in the army.

Many didn't have a job waiting for them back home either so I guess that would be another reason plus it will be a nice place now the fighting has stopped and when everything is back to normal.

All of the trophies and skins will be prepared and mounted over here and will be shipped back when they are finished.

I am so looking forward to returning home to catch up with you and all my old chums and settle down and start looking for a woman for my own wife, you know I was disillusioned with the war some time ago and I glad it is finally all over, who would have thought it has gone on for nearly another 2 years since we enlisted.

See you soon

My great love for you all

William (Bill)

Two days later Bill was waiting at his hotel as Louis rode up ' the 'boys' set off yesterday with one of the wagons and will have camp set up tonight when we catch up to them, the others and my second wagon have not long left this morning and we will pass them somewhere along the road, we are off'

That night they caught up to the first wagon and Bill and Louis sat down for a glass of whisky and a cigarette while the Blacks continued cooking the evening meal over a fire, they had stacked scrub around the encampment with an opening for the second wagon expected in another couple of hours and were singing a chant while a couple of them engaged in a shuffling dance.

'They will keep the fire going all night less there are any ranging Lions or Dogs around although they aren't generally this close to the town' Louis said 'but we will have to do this every night anyway so they may as well get used to it'

'Do they need a hand with anything' Bill asked

'We aren't going to help them, they are getting better pay than most of their type who aren't getting anything except a life in the mines and anyway we don't mix with them, they were slaves until about three years ago they are going to be well fed and kept, just relax until they have finished cooking one thing most of them can manage even without their women is how to cook and serve a good feed, they are happy and will be celebrating when you 'knock over' your first animals don't worry about them, they are bloody lucky I took them on!'

That night they sat at their table on the two chairs that had been bought for their use and had finished their meal which was as Louis had described and he was telling Bill about his childhood, his first experience with his childhood slaves and how he had killed his first Lion when he was nine years old 'I was more scared of my Father than the Lion and just wanted to get home, but I hated the bastard for making me may stay out there all night with a couple of Black kids for company and I made him pay when I was old enough' he added 'the Blacks thought I was a great hunter but I must admit I learnt a lot about keeping your nerve on that occasion and I was never short of company when I wanted to take some of them after that to

104

carry back the meat and trophies and I taught myself the skills by listening to and watching some of the older Blacks. Those jokers thought like the animals we were hunting sometimes, how they used to get big game with a couple of bloody sharp sticks I don't know but they were doing it long before we got here so you have to give them a bit of respect for that and I certainly learnt a lot from them' he grudgingly acknowledged.

'These boys are a mixture of Masai and Zulu, years ago they would have been killing each other but the war has treated them just as badly as everyone else. Although I don't have much to do with them you have to admire them as until about 50 years ago they ruled this country and especially the Zulu, we fought them on numerous occasions during the great Trek and they showed the British at Iswandlwana when they decimated them 'the first defeat of a modern army by an inferior indigenous people' he laughed. It wasn't until Rourkes drift when the Brits decided to use a bit of common sense and later when we joined with them that the Zulu were finally put in their place; both them and the Masai have been pretty good warriors and you admire them for that but they know their place now!' he concluded.

Bill reciprocated by telling him of the New Zealand experience and how all the game animals and a lot of fish and game birds had been introduced to replicate the hunting environment from the 'old' country, he explained how they had got established and how one needed a licence to hunt Deer, (Stags only and one per year) although there were plenty of Pigs and it was open slather against them. He described how his Father had been one of the influential property owners in the area and how he had funded part of the Acclimatisation Society work to resource and introduce new animals, birds and fish and always seemed to be successful every year in his application for a balloted license to shoot deer.

He also described the beauty of the rivers and mountains and how he missed his family and especially his younger sister who he hadn't seen for nearly two years now.

They were starting to establish some kind of rapport with each having a grudging respect for the other and as they went to their tents that night Louis said 'I nearly brought one of those English officers hunting, glad it didn't work out, you Colonials are better bushmen, shots and soldiers than they ever were and our war was going alright till you came along, you will be alright for company see you in the morning'

It was two days later after leaving the established roads and rail lines and entering into the veldt and travelling among old gullies, dried watercourses patches of scrub and the odd isolated tree or kopje that the going got a little more difficult.

The wagons were forced to manoeuvre around some of the obstacles and out of the old creek beds and the Blacks were often engaged on assisting with pushing and clearing around the wheels to keep them moving 'oxen are better in this country but they are a lot slower than horses and at least there's only two wagons' said Louis. Bill had offered to assist but the Blacks looked strangely at him and Louis said 'for Christs sake man, its their job to keep up and keep moving, just leave them to it'

After the first wagon had negotiated a difficult area it was always easier for the second wagon and horses until one event where the two wagons had been too close and were both stuck, one behind the other, and the natives were struggling to make any headway 'bugger this said Bill we have to hook up our horses as well to get some extra pull on the front wagon and we can help with a push' and he dismounted and began to tie his mount to the traces 'suit yourself' said Louis 'but I have no intention of helping the useless bastards, they got themselves into it and they can get themselves out, I am going to sit and watch'

After several more minutes the first wagon was getting in even worse strife and Bill stormed over 'get off your arse and give us a hand, we aren't going to progress if you don't buckle down and get in and help us, I don't care whether you like it or not' The Blacks were looking on silently, they hadn't heard an Afrikaaner spoken to like this and waited to see what would happen. Without a word Louis walked his horse to the front of the wagon and began to tie it to the traces and he then lent his considerable strength to the back of the wagon until finally it was free and within a few minutes the second wagon was similarly moved and they were ready to progress again.

He was having difficulty holding his rage and as they rode forward again he turned to Bill 'you won that round but don't ever talk to me in front of those Blacks like that again or you can keep your money and piss off' he added, inside knowing that he had committed most of the funds to this his first safari and really couldn't afford to call it off.

'Maybe I over reacted but look how we got it done when you gave a hand, maybe next time I won't have to ask and maybe you just help out sometimes, we are all in it together'

They rode in in virtual silence for the rest of the day, both of them inwardly thinking about the situation until that night when they were again sitting having a whisky while the evening meal was being prepared Louis said 'alright maybe I am a wee bit biased and maybe they actually aren't a bad lot of 'boys' all things considered 'and maybe you have a lot of guts talking to me like you did, lets forget it, it won't happen again you are right we may as well get on a bit, all of us.'

'Good on you it takes a man to admit when he is wrong I am not going to dwell on it anymore, have another whisky and another pipe' said Bill 'there's another day tomorrow'

In the afternoon of the next day they had seen large herds of game animals and decided they would make a stalk and see if they could bag the first trophy of the hunt and were readying to set off with two of the Blacks accompanying and the others busy establishing a base camp which was going to last them for a few days.

There were herds of Gemsbok ranging just in the distance and constantly hiding in the depressions and scrub, beyond them were Springbok and in the far distance Wildebeest, Zebra and, they thought Lions, all though they were hard to define in the heat haze and distance.

Louis half whispered 'The animals can smell water I reckon, and that's probably why there are so many here, we need to get within about a hundred metres and they are pretty wary, they seem to alternately feed and then keep watch so we have to be careful. You will either have to shoot them in the shoulder so you can get a cape for your mounted head or we will have to shoot a couple until we can get a clean cape in any case you want the biggest one which is in those animals to our left and there is a big female with those younger animals and other females' ' I think we are going to have to crawl the next two or three hundred metres to get close enough if I lift my hand stop and I will let you come forward as we get close enough'

And so the stalk began Bill had a nervous expectation and thrill as he carefully made his way forward, finally he was motioned forward as Louis whispered 'they are just forward of us, the big one is by that bush on the right take her'

Bill carefully sighted on the animal, held his breath and squeezed off the trigger on the 7x57mm Mauser rifle and watched as the beast crumpled to the ground, immediately there was a stampede of animals bursting out of cover and leaping and running from the area.

'A good clean shot' said Louis 'well done' behind them the Blacks were running to the scene cheering and in the distance another four were coming up from the camp with two horses. They arrived after some time and were as jubilant as Bill and they began leaping about with a another chant as they made their way to the animal, and then began to skin it out and dress it. Louis had taken a number of photos with Bills *'Brownie number 1 camera'* which had been issued during the war 'take plenty I have few rolls of film' was the instruction.

'Man you are going to get plenty of trophies yet, better save some film' was the reply.

That night the Blacks were happy as they had recovered the meat and the larger parts were suspended from a tripod frame and winch that had been on one of the wagons for this purpose 'we won't need any more meat for a while but if you get a Springbok we will take some of that, it's better eating anyway, the boys will dry some jerky for us and clean and salt the skin and I suggest tomorrow we will head off with four of the 'boys' following with a wagon and see if we can get Wildebeest and just maybe another animal in the evening, we are well set up now and they have a good barricade around the camp and we will keep a good fire going all night and they will take turns to keep a watch, we will have to return to camp each night its too dangerous to tent out here!'

That night Bill went to sleep in his tent dreaming of the days to come, remembering the thrill of his first big game animal on his safari and hearing the guttural grunts of Lions circling outside the camp and periodic shouts and beating of drums from the 'boys' to scare them off.

And so it was the next day with Bill and Louis again nearing the herd then crawling closer before Bill took a shot at his first Wildebeest, he had been instructed 'hit it just right behind the shoulder and it will go down, if it charges stand up, stand your ground and head shoot it, remember X marks the spot and line up the cross between its eyes and its horns when you shoot'. Bill was rapt when he saw the great beast fall to his well directed first shot as although he was confident he had had some reservations about standing in front of a charging animal weighing quarter of a ton or so.

Louis was pleased as well 'you can certainly shoot well, I give you that, another nice clean shot and you have yourself a great trophy there, that is as big as any I have seen and I have seen a lot' The 'boys' arrived with the wagon and horses and began the butchering task once again clapping and dancing with delight Bill thought they are really enjoying this and seem so happy in this environment, it had been cruel to lock the poor buggers behind barbed wire in the camps.

That evening they hadn't been able to stalk other game close enough for a shot and Bill was not going to try a long shot in case he only wounded an animal 'no problem' there is tonnes of time Louis said 'I haven't done this for about 3 years now and I am starting to enjoy it, I might even throw in an extra day if we need it, its bloody good to come out with another good hunter and I have to admit I am pleased you picked me'

'Don't get too carried away we might end up friends and that would never do considering we were trying to shoot each other about a month ago, what a stupid bloody war I lost my best mate who had joined up with me and he was going to bring out his fiancée and get married and live here until he was shot about four days after the bloody war was finished!' Bill said.

And so they continued hunting ranging each day from their encampment with several of the 'boys' dependent on which species they were hunting following behind with the horses and a wagon.

After another week Bill had acquired Zebra skins, Springbok and Gazelle and had decided he should take a trophy head and skin of the 'king of beasts' or in other words a Lion as his last act of the safari.

Louis explained how the males were usually quite sedentary and it was the females who normally did all the killing of other animals for food but it was the males that displayed all the aggression. He explained that a couple of Lions were usually no match for a pack of dogs or hyena and they commonly made a kill to promptly have it taken off them

They were usually to be found in areas with a bit of scrubby cover which they used to rest up in during the heat of the day and also as cover when they were stalking prey. The big males were often 'loners' and were poor hunters the only thing in their favour as a trophy was their size and the copious mane as they were often in bad condition and near starvation from being unable to hunt and resorting to eating vermin and scraps where they could find them, however this didn't make them any less dangerous when angered.

Accordingly they rode out on the horses accompanied by two of the 'boys' jogging alongside and they were constantly stopping where ever they could find a bit of elevated ground so that they could glass the area with binoculars in search of the trophy, and it was near midday when they located their quarry in a slight depression and clearing in the scrub with a couple of dead trees nearby.

After stalking for about an hour they were within shooting distance and Bill was told 'wait till it stands then shoot' as Bill took the shot a bird flew up beside him and he involuntarily flinched and pulled the shot slightly and to his horror the beast moved off into the long grass.

'We are in trouble now' said Louis 'but nothing to be done about it for a while, we will give it a few minutes to hopefully move away and die then go and find it, we will be able to follow the blood trail and I will have the 'boys' behind with spare guns ready loaded, we will take the shotguns because any shot now is going to be a short range and they are full of buckshot which will be better than a rifle in here!, hopefully its down anyway but just be careful you will have to lead off'

With some trepidation Bill began to follow the trail of blood which was bright red indicating a flesh wound the stalk was simple except visibility was limited to only a few feet in front and to each side, when suddenly there was a crash and the Lion leapt from the scrub and onto Bills shoulder with its claws while its teeth were clasping around the back of his neck. Bill collapsed under the weight and pain and heard the resounding boom of a shotgun as Louis had fired and he lay supine beneath the now dead beast.

Louis and the 'boys' pulled the dead Lion to one side and checked on Bill who was feeling decidedly unwell, the lacerations on his back and shoulders were bleeding profusely as were the bite marks around the back of his neck and he had gone into shock and was shaking uncontrollably.

He was loaded onto his horse and tied so he couldn't fall off and the team set off at speed to take him towards the camp.

Bill had come to back at the camp in considerable pain, the medical repairs consisted of the application of liberal parts of whisky over the cuts and lacerations as a sterilant and then the painful work of stitching up the worse areas, one of the older Blacks had prepared a poultice of ground leaves and barks which was applied and then bandaged over, a large shot of whisky had been administered as an anaesthetic during all this and in spite of requests for more he was advised 'no more for you until you have had a bit of rest and sleep'

Later that night Bill awoke to be told 'well you have a souvenir of a few scars and the boys have recovered your skin and the head for you so you can have an impressive floor mat for your house, you are lucky it jumped high on you so I could shoot it with the shotgun and the hole in the hide is now an added feature and you will be able to talk about it for years'

'We will rest up here for a few days or a week until you come right, we have plenty of food and provisions and we will make sure the poultices and stitching are all okay before I take you back to Pretoria, the boys have enjoyed your company and think you are an alright sort of a guy and I guess I do too so enjoy a few days on me'

'Thanks for that' replied Bill 'I can see now why we didn't import any of these bloody things while we were populating New Zealand with game animals' he laughed cringing with the pain and he muttered a response 'talk about it in the morning I need something to help me sleep'

'I have a little Laudanum which will help with the pain and you can have some more in the morning we will talk again then'

With a few days while Bill recovered the time was spent sitting outside smoking a few pipes together and swapping experiences and a great camaderie was being established with a mutual respect and liking for each other, Louis told of the time when he and Wilhelm had just left to join the rebels and they were chased and he was shot in the arse and described how they had shot and killed two of the pursuers before making an escape that night on one horse and how painful that had been.

'Believe it or not I think that was James and I that shot you , we were ahead of the English troops and let drive at you and we thought we had hit someone'

'Lucky you didn't tell me that before the Lion attacked you or I might have let him have you and even helped him a bit' Louis laughed and they talked about the poor English troops 'they rode up and stood there with their mounts after you had been firing in plain view and started talking to you while you were in half cover no wonder Wilhelm couldn't resist it and he told me he shot one of them off his horse and pulled off a good shot when he knocked another one off as they fled for cover, stupid buggers, you Colonials didn't do silly things like that it was almost as if they were asking to be shot, did they think it was all a game?'

They laughed over the event and Bill said at the time they had a grudging respect for the event although they would happily have killed both of them at that time, it was one of their first serious actions in the war and until then they had been destroying Boer homes, on 'drives' and looking after concentration camps all of them jobs both him and James had detested and Bill described how he especially had become a bit sick of the whole thing and the way the war was being carried out. He added his experience when they had sacked a farm and then he had met the wife in the concentration camp and how he had taken pity and given her some bread and had intended to look after her a bit with some extra food but how she had committed suicide within days as the last of her children died, 'that sickened me' he said 'the night before we had rested under the stars talking about the southern cross or your kite and shortly after Marie was dead, I just felt so sad that we had brought her to that despair and end'

'Did you say Marie, which camp, and where was the farm you had sacked?' Louis cried out 'where was it man?'

When Bill described the locations Louis was bereft; 'that was Wilhelm's farm and his wife you tried to help, I can't believe this it just seems so unreal that in the whole country you and Wilhelm had such a connection, he was a great friend of mine and Marie had already lost children in childbirth before the war and they only had two children, we knew that they had all died in the camps and Wilhelm was burning with a desire for revenge after we heard and was merciless in his approach to the war, we were out together with a small Kommando towards the end and he had set up separate from us in a sniping location and I was to collect him again that evening, unfortunately he had been shot and killed before I got back there which was a terrible shame as we later discovered the war had finished 4 days before'

Bill recoiled thinking 'surely it just couldn't be true that they had all been so connected that James had been shot and killed by Wilhelm it was just inconceivable that he, Bill, had borne such hatred for someone who had been Marie's Husband' he decided that there had been enough pain and hatred in the damned war and to keep his counsel and say no more about it. He was just amazed at the fact they had come half way around the world to a province of

Transvaal, about the same size as the British Isles, and established connections three times with the same people, it was almost the stuff of legends and fairy tales.

Louis hardly noticed but was musing 'it's a bad thing when you think about it a whole family gone for nothing at the end, the wars over now and I am not even sure who won in the end, we lost a bit of independence and a whole lot of people have died, my homeland has been destroyed what was it all for?' he posed the question to Bill.

'I certainly don't know, we set off full of honour and duty to the Queen, she has died during the war anyway, and looking for a bit of adventure and I certainly aren't proud of some of the things that have been done and like you I wonder what it was all for?'

It was several days later when they finally decided Bill was able to travel and they teamed up after removing the camp and packing everything into the wagons and set off on their way back towards Wanderfontein and then Pretoria where Bill would return to New Zealand and Louis would look for another client.

Near Wanderfontein

20th June 1902

Der Mater, Pater and Millicent

My last letter from South Africa and hopefully it gets to you before I am home.

I have finished our hunting trip and have a large number of trophies to adorn our home when they arrive back in New Zealand

The hunting has been great and although we didn't hit it off at first I have enjoyed the company and time with our previous enemy, Louis is a fine man and I would like to think I have 'knocked a few rough edges' off him and he seems a bit more tolerant towards his natives than when we set off.

Looking forward to finally being home with you all

I will post this letter when we reach Elandsfontein

Love Bill (William)

Their entourage stopped and made camp about 2 days from Wanderfontein and they were camped off to the side of a disused rail siding for the night when two Australians with horses and a wagon rode up to their camp 'hello there, we are John Murphy and David Reilly, do you mind if we take camp with you tonight' they were asked.

'Pull up and tie off your mounts and come and have a whisky with us' they were told 'the boys are making our supper and you are welcome to share, I am Louis and this is my train and my client Bill from New Zealand'

Chapter 16 : After the War

David O'Reilly and John Murphy - the Australians

Pretoria June 1902

The war is over and our two Australian heroes David and John are in Pretoria.

Yesterday they signed out of the Bushmen Carbineers and received their final pay. They also have a copy of a letter from a grateful British commander for the efforts of their force in the conflict and a recognition of their service in the advice a special medal will be struck for all who have served.

Being volunteers in an informal independent force means that they were not subject to army discipline, although they had operated under military systems and have no formal duty after the conflict has ended.

'All we have to do is get to Elandsfontein with some horses and provisions, head down the siding rail line to our location, pick up the gold and we are rich !'

'I can hardly wait man lets go and have a well earned beer or two first, although this bloody stuff is like water and doesn't knock you about, I can't wait till we get home and into some dinkum Aussie beer I say' added John.

And so it was they found themselves in a back street bar regaling other Australian ex troops, New Zealanders on leave or who had signed out, a few British (a mixture of English, Scots and Irish) with a few despondent Boers in the background, and anyone else who would listen 'we showed everybody how it should be done, they should have just got a heap of us Australians here in the first place and it would have been over a couple of years ago, too much pussy footing around, you had to be hard and show no mercy to the bastards' they mouthed.

'It's a bloody shame about our 'Breaker Morant' as well, bloody English bastards getting him shot just for saving their faces, the Minister shouldn't have interfered and he would still be alive, his own stupid fault, have another beer John me mate and lets drink to him, the bravest in the Australian Bushman Carbineers, the bravest soldiers in the British Empire which cannot be disputed, every one have a drink with us to the glorious Bushman Carbineers' David roared lifting his glass towards the ceiling in a wild swing.

David and John were alone in their toast and most of the others had turned their backs to them and were talking among themselves 'that's right all you bastards, ignore us and our great deeds, next time fight your own bloody war' John called out.

Two of the Boers got up to walk out, great big bearded men; now the war was over there was a tolerance towards them and a grudging admiration for their struggle tempered with a hatred by some who lost their friends and colleagues during the war, however a recognition that 'war is war' and all in the room had just left them to drink in peace.

There was a silence across the room as they headed towards the door and as the bar waited to see what would happen next 'bugger off then, can't take the truth you lot are the bastards that started the war and you got your lesson so piss off' John said as they walked past, John was full of a confidence and arrogance imbued by the copious amounts of beer they had drunk to this time.

'You lot come to our country, destroy our farms, imprison and kill our women and children and call that a war, I call you a bunch of cowards hiding behind your British Empire, come outside and we will show you who can fight around here, we have had to listen to you two all afternoon and we are sick of it'

The rest of the bar may have been tolerant of the Boers but there was no way they were going to allow their Australian allies get beaten up by a couple of the previous enemy and two Scots rose to their feet 'listen tae us, you'll not take them ootside, they are in no condition tae fight anyway so just leave, they are full of the drink and don't know a half of whit they are saying anyhoo, away with ye' one of them said.

'Alright but they better hope they don't meet us again when they are sober as we will 'knock their blocks off' was the response as the two left.

'That showed the bastards, they didn't worry us anyway we would have given them a bloody good hiding and sent them on their way with their tail between their legs if you two hadn't interfered but thanks anyway' John slurred as he swayed about on his unsteady feet.

'you should go home and sleep it off' someone called out 'you have outstayed your welcome anyway its time you were off' one of the English soldiers added.

'These are our Australian mates and you don't talk to them like that while we are here you bloody English Git' called on of the other Australian drinkers 'they are right we did come over and finish your war for you lot'

Things were getting a bit heated until a punch was thrown and next minute the bar erupted into a brawl between the Australians and New Zealanders and the rest while the remaining Boers were still seated at the rear watching the action.

Neither side seemed to be gaining any advantage although there were a couple of bodies now prone on the floor when the barman fired a shot into the air bringing hostilities to a halt . He brandished the shotgun 'it has one more barrel , take your scrap outside, or one of you is going to get an arse full of birdshot' he ordered 'or just sit down again and calm down, your choice'

Although a couple went outside to continue their individual battles the majority sat down again at the tables muttering and complaining but considering honour had been satisfied.

David and John continued haranguing anyone else that would listen and continuing in the previous vein until within an hour they collapsed at the bar in a drunken stupor clutching to one another and bearing the scars and scrapes of the recent scrap.

The barmen took great pleasure in lifting the inert forms, carrying them to the door and tossing them into the street to the general applause of the rest of the room.

It was several hours later and dark, except for a faint glow from the bar windows where it was being cleaned; when David awoke, he shook John until he also came to 'what happened' were his first words, 'I remember a fight but I thought it had finished how did we end up out here? We had better make our way back to our rooms if we can remember where they are'

They staggered to their feet and holding one another up began to trudge down the street unsure where they were headed but hoping to recognize a landmark somewhere.

It was only about another few hundred metres when John sensed someone was following them and as he turned to look back he was felled by a blow to the head. He lay on the ground as David almost instantly joined him and suddenly they were being kicked with heavily booted feet.

He felt his jaw crack and thought his ribs must be broken as several more kicks were delivered and to his side he could see that David was not being treated any better and was moaning and begging for the attack to stop.

Finally the two assailants stopped and one of them said 'go home Australians, you aren't wanted here, if we see you again you are dead' and John recognised the Afrikaans tongue in the message and realised who were their assailants. They were ungraciously stripped of their wallets and watches plus tobacco and pipes and were abandoned as they lay.

In spite of the pain they dropped off again and it wasn't until the next morning they were discovered and picked up and loaded to a wagon and taken to the nearest Military Hospital to be told 'although you aren't actually part of the military we have been told you served in the forces here, we will fix you up but it going to take a while, you both have a number of broken ribs which have been strapped and will heal shortly but you John have a fractured jaw, we have wired it up but you won't be eating for a while and it will take at least 2 weeks before its even likely to be setting plus we think you might have some internal injuries along with your partner who we know has a broken arm as well, you have that much alcohol still in your system you can't have any pain relief for at least a day until it wears off, after that we will check every day until you leave'

David whispered 'I wish we had just headed off towards Wanderfontein, now we have no money for horses or provisions and are likely to be here for a few weeks and I think I have something crook inside as well, how are you feeling mate?' The response was a desolate look of despair and a nod which he assumed was agreement as John rolled over to rest in agony from pain with his left shoulder and right side below his ribs.

By the next morning John has had internal bleeding and a collapsed blood pressure which have seen emergency surgery for a ruptured spleen and David has also been discovered to have a broken sternum with more wrapping and requiring total rest, after about three days however he is slowly starting to make some recovery and is proving a handful for Doctors with his refusal to rest and for the Nurses with his often risqué and downright rude requests for additional services. Throughout this time John is in almost continual pain and is starting to wonder how they could ever have been childhood and adult friends when he is just such a bloody nuisance and a pain in the bum!

Finally after a couple of weeks they are both well on the road to recovery and starting to ask when they might be released from the hospital Johns broken jaw has recovered and he can eat again with difficulty although he has been told he will have a crooked smile for the rest of his life which will only be worsened by the considerable number of teeth he has lost as well. His spleen injury is on the mend and his ribs are losing their soreness, David has on the contrary been moving about after only the first few days in spite of instructions to rest and allow his sternum and ribs to set properly and has proved a big nuisance to all and sundry, however he refuses to leave until 'my mate can come with me, we have important business out there waiting'

Finally one month later they are again on the street but his time penniless and they make their way to a hostel which has been established for displaced persons like themselves.

'Mate we have hit rock bottom now, we just have to get to our gold somehow and it will all be OK again, no more beer or drink this time until we get our hands on it and we are safely back in the city again!' David vows.

'Well we won't work for it, that's for suckers and no one is going to give it to us, so we are just going to have to take it, ever robbed anything?' John asks.

'What do you suggest, I suspect we better not try a mugging anyone, an old lady with an Umbrella could out fight us both right now plus we haven't got any weapons, horses or even a bloody mask, you better have a good idea ?'

'We go for a bank' John was in his element 'we don't need guns, no one questions a gun when its pointed at you so we make some wooden ones, steal a couple of horses, they are all over the place these days and once we have the money we leave town as fast as we can and make our way towards the east, simple really, all we have to do is select which bank we are going to hit and it's all on for us'

David had some considerable reservations about the whole thing but couldn't think of an alternative, they could go to the 'doss' house but that was only a short term option, they were too knocked about to work so maybe John's idea was the way to go. That afternoon saw them sitting on the riverbank with their pocket knives whittling away at a couple of forked sticks and making a semblance of a revolver each and when they were finished they compared the finished product ' if the customers are blind we will be successful, they don't look much like a real gun to me" David opined.

'We have got to get a fire and blacken them and see if we can get a bit of a shine on them, you really don't want to show them too much but I reckon they will do the job, lets finish them off and see what tomorrow brings, remember the spirit of our famous Bushranger Ned Kelly and have confidence that's what will win through, the spirit of Australia' laughed John 'the worst that can happen is we get looked after in Jail for a bit and suffer a bit of delay'

'A bit of delay? they will throw us in Jail for a few years for attempted bank robbery if it doesn't work out, there must be some other way'

'Well I would like to hear it then, pull yourself together it will be a bit of a hoot, we only want enough for a stake to go and get the gold and it will all be pretty simple, there are plenty of banks been robbed before!' John said 'now let's go and have some tucker at the free kitchen and then we'll come back here and light a fire and continue with our guns and get some charcoal to blacken our guns and our faces' 'tomorrow we will go and sort out a bank, tomorrow night we will flog a couple of horses and kit and we will hit the bank the following day then we are off!'

And so they continued refining their wooden guns that evening back at their camp and after a meal at the kitchen until they looked fairly realistic and then used some of the charcoal to blacken the wood and give a semblance of steel colour to the pieces before going to sleep under the bridge which they had made a rudimentary home since leaving the hospital.

Next morning they walked around some of the outer suburbs of Pretoria seeking out a small enough branch of a bank that they could realistically rob and finally settled on an area in the northern part of the city with a branch of the Nedbank which seemed to suit their purpose. Although they dare not go inside they could ascertain from outside it had one old guard armed with a shotgun who sat at a chair near the entrance, with the shotgun leaning on the wall alongside him, one Teller behind a counter and a Managers office off to one side. The bank itself had a handy alley down one side where they decided they could tie up the horses before their escape and they had determined the best way to head out of town and all that remained was to acquire the horses that evening and be ready to go next morning.

The plan was to darken their faces with the charcoal, while in the alley draw up their handkerchiefs as a mask during a period when there were no pedestrians near nor customers in the bank, over power the guard and take his shotgun which immediately would give them a real firearm, one of them would hold the guard and manager captive while the other would get the money from the teller; a simple strategy and almost foolproof.

That evening they snuck into a stables after they thought the hostler had left for the night and picked two good looking mounts, stole a saddle and tack each and slowly and watchfully opened the stable door and led the horses onto the street. 'where do you think you are going' was the cry and a shotgun rang out as our heroes leapt onto the horses as they progressed at high speed down the street, others had rushed onto the street and hearing the yell 'stop horse thieves' a further barrage of shots was thrown towards them and several were already swinging their horses to give chase.

A frantic race ensued with both David and John suffering from the pace and the horses which were proving to be a little unruly and unaccustomed to the riders so they were having to wrestle with them as well, finally after a series of evasions they finally settled to a canter heading towards the bridge and their makeshift dwelling. 'Looks like we have left them behind some where I have just about had enough of this robbing caper already, we could have been shot there' David moaned 'I feel like I have just been through a wringer as I am sore all over, are you sure this is a good idea ?'

'Hell yes, that was the hard part, we now have everything for the morning and this time tomorrow night we will be on our way with a few Pounds to keep us going it's all easy from here on in, I must admit I am a bit sore as well but we will be right cobber after a good sleep'

The next morning they rose and began to prepare for the day, 'check you have your toy gun, mask, and saddle properly girthed and we will make our way into the city and then towards our bank, we will check it out until the street is empty and there are no customers and then we will get our funds to carry on'

They duly made their way to the street and then the alley where they proceeded to hobble the horses 'use a slip knot we want to be able to move fast after we come out and no one except in the bank will even know we were here' was the instruction.

When all was clear they pulled up their handkerchiefs and burst into the Bank brandishing their wooden pistols and David turned towards the Guard 'don't move old man or you are a dead man' he threatened as he reached across for the shotgun.

'You are no black man that's only charcoal on your face and that gun is just a piece of wood' called out the Guard.

David grabbed the shotgun by the barrel and drew it across the seated Guard who reached out to grab it, next minute there was a retort 'boom' as one barrel discharged. 'you bloody old bastard let go' screamed David as he was frantically tugging at the weapon and finally stood erect with the shotgun in his grasp ' now get over there' he ordered 'and shut up or you are in big trouble' he threatened.

'For Christ sake get a move on that shot will have woken up half the bloody street and get them over there.' 'You' he said to the watching Teller ' load all the money from your till into a money bag and be quick about it' waving his wooden gun around forgetting that the Teller would now be aware it was just a toy and he watched with dismay as he sunk below the counter 'get up and get our money blast you' he screamed out ' David leave them and come here with that shotgun and blast away this catch and I will go and get the money myself'

'can't, we only have one shot left in the shotgun' was the response.

John leapt over the counter and dragged the Teller to his feet 'get over there and stay quiet, if he moves shoot him' he ordered as he dragged the till open, in his hurry he pulled it beyond its stop and next minute the floor was strewn with the coins and notes from the till.

Swearing and cursing he frantically began to pick up and load the cash into a Teller bag off the counter 'come and help' he ordered the Teller 'this is all your fault, hurry up, where's all the rest?'

'This is all the spare cash we have today, no one comes in until tomorrow after the stock sales' the Teller advised helping to load the bag. He was beginning to get a bit of confidence realizing that the our two robbers were almost at a disadvantage with three people against them in the Bank and them only armed with one shot in a shotgun and two wooden guns 'I don't suppose you do this very often?' he queried ' doesn't seem like a very professional job to me' he snorted with a grin developing on his face.

'Don't you get smart with me' retorted John 'right that's it' and he ran to the counter door opened it and said to David 'lets scarper'

They ran out of the Bank and turned towards the horses and the alley to see three mounted Armed Constabulary riding at speed down the street towards them and a number of people watching from the sidewalks to see what was going on. John grabbed the shotgun from David and fired at the approaching horsemen who pulled their mounts to a stop and took cover behind a trough and began to fire their pistols at our robbers!'

John and David leapt to the horses and lashed them to a gallop bending over the neck as they headed away. 'They haven't got any weapons, go and catch them' yelled out the Bank Manager who had rushed onto the street 'get up and go quickly' he was calling to the Constabulary.

Within minutes the chase was on amid the firing from the pursuing trio 'shall, we just surrender now?' was the question. 'Keep going they will never hit us with a revolver at this speed and something will turn up' was the reply albeit not particularly confidently.

They progressed towards the limits of the city with the Constabulary in hot pursuit and continually firing at them when they viewed a rail crossing in the distance

'The train is 100 yards away and so are we and they are 100 yards behind, it's all an omen' yelled John 'let's go in front of the train and we will leave them behind'

'What if we can't make it?' David yelled.

'Well you won't have to worry for too long, keep going' was the response and with a final spurt they headed for the crossing and the approaching train. 'we are doing 20 miles an hour and the train is doing about 30 miles an hour but we are slightly closer to the crossing therefore we will be okay by my calculation, and you can have my share of the money if I am wrong' John shouted.

They crossed the tracks with a split second and what felt like inches to spare, in the midst of the shrieking whistle of the train and the grinding of the wheels on the track as it was trying to slow down. David would have sworn the draught as it went by had almost blown him from the saddle.

'We have a few minutes now till it goes past and they can follow, let's get as far away as we can, ride as hard as you can' was the cry.

Towards midday and they slowed to a canter 'I think we have lost them and we are safe from pursuit pull up and we will take a breather' said John 'you couldn't get anything more exciting than that if you tried' he laughed with an underlying sense of relief 'someone up there is looking after us, I don't think we could have done anything more wrong and still got away with it'

David was certainly beginning to feel considerable relief himself 'I guess you are right, certainly filled in the morning' he laughed.

They sat under the shade of some bush and decided to count their new funds before moving off again towards Wanderfontein and then their gold and it didn't take a lot of time 'for risking our lives or imprisonment we have the great sum of two pounds and fourteen shillings plus some small change, that should keep us going for at least two days or so!' 'what a great success!' David said and they both began to laugh and roll about on the ground 'I can't wait for your next bright idea we only have a few days and several hundred miles to go at this rate we will be robbing a bank every two days' he added to more uncontrolled laughter probably brought on by a relief after their experience. 'perhaps we rob a train' he added to more hoots of laughter 'I hope you didn't throw away your wooden gun' and they convulsed again on the ground shaking with glee and relief.

That night their horses escaped as they had not been hobbled properly 'we had better try and get a ride on the road' they agreed

Meantime in the City, the Chief of the Constabulary is doing a bit of research and detective work. 'they were white men and sounded to me like Colonials possibly Australians from the twang in their talk and one of them was called David pretty strong looking chaps although they didn't move fast as though they were a bit sore from something, might have been injured in the war perhaps, certainly had plenty of cheek having us on with a couple of wooden guns' said the bank staff as they were interviewed.

His next investigation was to check with the Australian Army records via their quartermaster who checked on those Australians who had left the army and were not intending to return to Australia; although he had a couple of Davids and one John it didn't take long to establish they were still in Pretoria and ,in fact, working as Armed Constabulary so it was obvious they were not regular Australian soldiers so he went to the Colonel who had commanded the Bushman Carbineers 'do you know a couple of chaps David and John who might have been with your command and who hang out together' he was asked 'yes I do, there were only about 230 of them and I remember two joined together, full of cheek and confidence, just wait and I will look them up for you' it was only a few minutes later when he advised 'we had David O'Reilly and John Murphy ex army but joined us together after living in South Africa and joined the Bushman Carbineers but left a month ago when the war ended, although we were army we weren't part of the regular force so they were just paid out but a medal is going to be struck for all of them, here is where they were going to stay at least the first night away, we also have a photograph taken when they enlisted with us and a next of kin for both of them'

It didn't take long to discover that although they had booked in at the Hotel they had never stayed the night so the Chief wondered if they had had an accident remembering the statement that they looked as though they may have been wounded and so on checking the Hospital he had solved the identity of the Bank robbers and everything about them except where they intended to go next. Their description photograph, names, height, weight, colour of their eyes, injuries and a mass of information was prepared and circulated throughout the Transvaal area by telegraph to all stations and the hunt was on with a nominal 50 pound reward for information leading to capture.

Meanwhile David and John have spent the night camped in an old railway hut alongside the main line and have just woken up 'at least we got away unscathed , the charcoal might not have been the best disguise, but at least no one will know who we are!' said John 'I reckon we spend the two pound which should buy us a pistol and next time rob a bar, a decent one must have better takings than that bloody waste of a bank, I can't believe it only had about a decent weeks work in the whole till'

'I have to agree' John said 'lets go across to the road and wait for a traveller or a wagon and see if we can buy a pistol off one of them'

They duly approached the road and started walking East towards Elandsfontein 'we may as well, have to end up in that direction anyway'

It was later that morning when two riders came along the road riding two horses and with another two mounts pulling a laden wagon 'gooday there, where have you two come from, and what are you up to' called out one of the riders.

'We are trying to get to Wanderfontein and hitched a ride on a train to save a bit of money but got caught and kicked off last night, we slept in that railway hut back there and looking for a bit of a hand, we are Australians and served with the Carbineers and thought we would try our hand at a bit of gold prospecting' David responded.

'I thought most of the gold is West and South of Pretoria, but I suppose you know what you are doing, we are Canadians and are staying on, we are just having a decent look around the place before we head back to Canada in July, didn't really get much of a look charging all over the place with the army and have a few bob so on the road for a while' ' we are heading your way so hop on the back of the wagon and rest your feet, I am Richard and this is my mate Roger, we have been through less than 6 months here together' after the introductions were finished they hopped onto the back and away they went.

And so they progressed 'do we knock up these two and flog the horses and just make off from here instead, what do you think?' asked John 'sounds like they have some money as well !'

'Never look a gift horse in the mouth mate, this is almost providence and meant to be, wait till tonight and we will see what is to be done, we don't want to have to knock them around if we can help it, seem a decent couple of chaps, maybe use what money we have to get them drunk then act from there, the Lord will provide he is obviously looking after us specially!'

And so that night they stopped at a small village on their way and after dinner decided to have a few drinks at the local bar 'we will shout you as it's only fair seeing as you two are giving us a ride' said John and so the evening began with our two intrepid Australians determined not to drink as much as their new Canadian friends until late that night they retired to their camp. It wasn't long before the two Canadians dropped into deep alcohol induced sleep which was what David and John had been waiting for and they then proceeded to lift their wallets taking what money they could find, despite the drunken protestations of one of the Canadians who had semi realized what was happening but soon silenced after they bound both of them , they also took a pistol and rifle each with ammunition and left the scene on the two horses and travelling again towards their destination.

It was later that morning when the two Canadians Richard and Roger finally broke free from their bindings and went to the local station in town to report their loss to the two thieves.

'Wait a minute' they were asked 'we have just received a telegram about two bank robbers, does this look like them?' "It doesn't just look like them it is them, John Murphy and David O'Reilly the thieving bastards, they are heading towards Wanderfontein when we picked them up and it looked this morning as though that's where they were heading from the marks they left' 'Right we will get to the Telegraph station and advise the settlements along the way, advise Pretoria and Wanderfontein, and we should be able to get them and get your things back for you'

It was later that day when a revised notice was advised and being printed on posters increasing the reward for capture or information leading to capture to one hundred pounds, the description included "Wanted Dead or Alive for Bank robbery, Horse and Property Theft – both armed and dangerous, approach with caution"

David and John confidently rode into the next town later that day and decided to buy some food and have a look around for a while until they spied a notice affixed to a street pole 'Christ that's us, with a fifty quid reward, I'm nearly tempted to turn you in myself' John laughed 'but really it's not very funny, we better buy our stuff and a bit extra and head across country before someone recognises us and decides he is going to make himself some money and we had better be quick about it'

That evening finds them camped North of the main road and rail line on the edge of the veldt camped around a small fire to provide a cooking means and a bit of warmth and protection from wild animals 'gets more risky by the day this life of crime however if we stay to the North we should come to the rail siding sometime and then we are close to the gold, the sooner the better this is hard on the nerves!' David volunteered and John had to agree. 'Yes mate you could say we are pushing our luck but the Lord looks after Catholics and so far so good, just a few days now surely and we are rich then just have to figure a way out of this country, I guess keep heading East or North to one of the other countries, German East Africa might be our best bet they don't like the Brits at all and we can find a way home from there'

The next day finds them out on the open veldt making their way towards the North, they have had to avoid a pride of Lions who didn't seem very interested in them but are getting concerned about a large pack of wild dogs which seem to be constantly trailing them from a distance 'someone told me these bloody things are the biggest threat in the South African countryside, they are certainly one of the ugliest and they just seem to be content staying their distance from us' David volunteered.

Later that afternoon they have dogs on each side of them plus behind and even some outliers running in front of them ' bastard things, there must be about fifty or more of the bloody things, let's make a camp and hope they come in a bit closer and we can despatch a few with our rifles and hopefully disperse them, where the bloody hell are we anyway, this country all just looks the same I guess we are still heading roughly north by the sun but I am not too happy about these dogs' and with that they pull to a halt near a small scrub patch and begin to find materials for a fire and to surround their camp while the wild dogs circle and still won't come close enough for a shot.

Its' not until evening, with their fire blazing and the horses tethered beside them that some of the dogs begin to venture closer, they are low to the ground as though foraging and constantly moving about as they near the encampment. 'right let's see if we can scare them away, take one each' so they have a good rest and sight on the dogs and squeeze off, one of them has been hit and the others wheel and retreat again to stand watching until a couple move in and begin to drag the carcase of the now dead dog away until suddenly there is about twenty dogs tearing at the carcase in a frenzy of eating 'they are bloody cannibals as well just fire into the heap of them we must get some more' John cries and let go several rounds each but are dismayed to discover they haven't hit a single animal 'must be further away than it looks' is the rueful comment 'we had better check our ammunition I am not sure how much we have and we better make a plan how to get out of here tomorrow'

It was a restless night with the dogs circling ever closer and the horses becoming restless and having to be constantly calmed throughout the night, they have had thirty rounds of ammunition between them and have been firing one round about every hour to keep the animals at bay but have been unable to hit another dog all night, they have lined up the Southern Cross in the night sky and determined the direction to travel South East until they can again locate the main road and rail line towards Wanderfontein and in the morning after a sleepless night they head in that direction and that afternoon they finally locate the rail line and head north following the line until with some relief they sight a small station in the distance about ten miles away. With one last fusillade of shots at the wild dogs they ride into the sanctuary of a small outpost with a station and perhaps another ten buildings but more importantly an open sided building set up as a bar!

They went into the bar and had a well earned cold beer while looking about them 'last time we got stuck into this we got into trouble and right now I reckon we have had enough, lets have just a couple and then we will see about getting us and our horses on a train, I think we need a guide with a few others to venture out into this open country again, it was alright when there was about 500 of you at a time but not so flash when you are by yourself.' David said.

'Too right and then we will bugger off to pick up the gold and then I am finished with this part of the country for good' was the response. 'with the few quid we have from our bank robbery but more importantly what we got from those Canadians we have got about thirty pounds that should be enough and after that we don't need to worry any more'

The next day saw our Australian pair on the train, luckily avoiding being identified by the station master, and heading to Wanderfontein where they duly dismounted that evening, collected the horses and went to a local stables to overnight them.

As they walked towards a hotel David grabbed John's arm 'look on that window! , we are wanted Dead or Alive and the reward is up to a hundred pound, we had better be careful and get this over with as soon as we can, we will book in , have dinner and get away at first light tomorrow'

During dinner they have been talking to a couple of locals and have told them about being pursued and harassed by Wild Dogs 'they usually won't attack two people on horses but you are safer with a wagon as the size will deter them but it's unlikely they would have attacked anyway' they are told.

In the far corner of the restaurant, and in the shadows, the two Canadians Richard and Roger were watching, they had managed to get the train to the City and had contacted some mates of theirs who had lent them some funds until they could find work 'we aren't going to take them here let's see where they go in the morning and follow, we will get our chance soon. I say we kill both of them, the bastards, robbing a man when he has tried to help them plus the hundred pounds is Dead or Alive and its simpler then looking after them' Richard mouthed.

The next morning David and John have collected their stolen horses purchased a wagon and gear and are on their way out of Wanderfontein heading along the old rail siding to the North and behind them keeping out of sight they are being followed by Richard and Roger 'we will just stay back and bide our time, I don't know where they are going but they must have something in mind, we follow until we find out what they are after, and then when we can get a chance to take them we will have our horses back and the reward money as well' they have decided.

On the second day towards evening they watch as David and John pull up with their wagon and dismount at a substantial camp with several wagons and a number of Blacks working about the camp and at least two other white men.

'That's too big for us we might have waited too long' Richard says 'let's make our way North to those old damaged and burnt out wagons in the distance and sit it out for a bit and see what tomorrow brings, we can watch through the binoculars in the morning and see if they are going to split up or carry on with that train of wagons'

Chapter 17

The Final Chapter

'All the worlds a stage, and all the men and women merely players: they have their exits and their entrances -------'

Monologue from 'As you like it' William Shakespeare.

And so our players take up their places.

Several miles North and East of Elandsfontein Louis Badenhorst, a Boer turned big game hunter, and Bill Gibson, an ex. New Zealand soldier, are encamped on their journey returning from a hunting trip towards Wanderfontein from where Bill intends to return to New Zealand and Louis to find another hunting client. They are established in a camp, with Louis' native helpers and his several horses and wagons, which is near a disused siding rail line from Wanderfontein.

With them are David O'Reilly and John Murphy who with their mounts and a wagon have been following the disused rail line and this evening have joined the camp. They are on their way, and in fact, are at the valley where during a battle and subsequent pursuit of Boers they had killed two Boer soldiers transporting Gold and Pounds in a wagon; they had discovered and buried the hoard and then fired the wagon and were now on their way to recover the bullion. On their journey to this point they had served with the Australian army and then the Australian Carbineers (a volunteer force) and so far had robbed a bank and two Canadians on their journey post the war to this point. They had a reward for their capture 'Dead or Alive' of one hundred pounds, a not insubstantial amount in those days and obviously due to their having been bush for about the last month Louis and Bill have no knowledge of this.

Some way distant and concealed from sight are Richard Kelly and Roger Byrne, two Canadian soldiers on leave who are pursuing the Australians for the reward and the return of their property which had been stolen from them by the two miscreants. They do not know that the meeting and encampment of the four whites is accidental and are biding their time until they can ascertain the next moves of their quarry. They have spent the night camped further up the valley beside another of the old abandoned and wrecked Boer wagons and with a favourable breeze blowing up the valley and behind some additional shelter of a Donga they had been able to light a small fire which they had kept going through the night.

That morning Louis is tending to the horses accompanied by Bill and the 'boys' are cooking a breakfast and beginning to break camp.

'We will have breakfast with them and wait until they head off before we go and find our gold, its just up this valley, I saw the distinctive hill as we rode up the siding and I think I can see in the distance the ruins of some wagons' David mouthed to John.

'I am pretty sure you are right, this is the spot alright, not long now and we will be rich and on our way out of this country and off' was the response.

Shortly the four of them have set down to a prepared breakfast and are discussing the day to come. In the interests of diplomacy and possibly because of the imposing size of Louis there has been no talk of the war since David and John have arrived and this morning is not going to be any different although each of them knows that the others have been involved in some way. Bill had shown the Australians some of his trophy heads and they had expressed an interest and suggested to Louis that they may well engage his services themselves sometime.

This had certainly sparked Louis' attention and he was discussing rates, timing etc completely unaware that they were 'spinning' him a line and had no intention of ever coming back near him.

'What are you doing here' he queried the Australians again 'you said last night you were prospecting but I have never heard of any gold discoveries anywhere near this end of the country, are you sure you aren't on a wild goose chase?'

'We have searched for gold in Australia and your country and we came here during the war and some of these formations around here look like they might be gold bearing, we are pretty experienced in prospecting and mining and have money from when we were paid out' they said tongue in cheek 'so we are going to have a fossick for several days, if it doesn't pan out we will try somewhere else'

'Well good luck to you but you would be better advised to follow us out to Wanderfontein and think of something else to do' Louis expounded 'Winter is coming and its going to get mighty cold at nights soon, don't say you weren't warned'

'Don't worry we know all about the cold up here alright, thanks for your advice you never know we might be back sooner than you think and rich as well!' was the response.

An hour later and both parties have finished their packing up and Louis' team of supply wagons have already left in advance and they are preparing to follow on their horses 'well good luck chaps, we might see you again, have fun' and Bill and Louis mounted their horses and began to follow the train of wagons.

'Thank Christ, I thought they were never going to leave, lets get our own wagon on the way and off we go' so saying, David whipped their horses into a slow canter and they moved off away from the rail line and towards the wrecked Boer wagons in the distance.

They made slow progress, searching after they were about a mile from the rail siding and trying to recognise exactly where they had been when they had pursued the Boers from the rail siding those months ago and looking for the evidence of the wagon they had fired, by now they were both walking and leading one of them was leading the horses as the other ranged to each side. The wind had blown some of the sandy soil in the valley and some of the light scrub had blown about making the search a little more difficult than they had envisaged.

Moving toward them under cover of a Donga and the patches of scrub in the area Richard and Roger, the Canadians are observing the Australians.

'At least we know they weren't a part of that other group, looks like they just overnighted with them' Roger said 'What the hell are they doing now? There must be something special they are looking for, we'll just bide our time and stay in cover until we can see what they are up to' he added.

'I've found it!' was the cry from David a couple of hours later ' here is the burnt out wagon and the wheel we had laid over the gold, its got to be' as he looked around trying to orientate himself and recall the area.

'By Jingo, you are right this is the spot!' responded John 'well done, let's start digging'

In the Donga Richard and Roger are watching on, they have neared the two Australians and are now only about 200 metres from them and watch as they are digging into the ground near the wreckage of a wagon, similar to where they had sheltered last night but this one a burnt out shell.

'I know its Dead or Alive' whispered Roger ' but we can't just shoot them down from here, that would be a cowards way, we will just take them alive and hand them over for the reward when we get back to town, we will get a bit closer and I will walk over and take them and you follow and back me up'

Several minutes later and they are within a 100 metres of the still scratching and digging Australians, Roger stands to his feet, raises his rifle and walks towards the pair 'alright you two, stop what you are doing and get up and raise your hands' he calls out.

The response is completely unexpected as they drop to the ground and begin frantically trying to make the shelter of their wagon and retrieve their guns. Richards answer to this action has been to loose a shot at them and he sees David slump flat to the ground while Roger has also fired but his shot has missed.

John has found the shelter of the wagon and grabs his rifle frantically chambering a shell he sights on Roger and fires. The force of the shot is like a hammer blow and Roger collapses clutching at his chest while blood spurts from the wound.

Richard is firing rapidly now but John is secure within the protection offered by the wagon and he fires back at Richard forcing him to cover again.

In the distance and perhaps three or four kilometres distant, Louis and Bill have heard the echoes of shots back where they have come from although they are pretty muted they can still recognize rifle fire when they hear it.

'I don't like the sound of that' says Bill 'the only people back there were those two we left a couple of hours ago, we should go back and check it out, won't take long'

'Christ Bill, lets just leave it' Louis says until he sees his resolute look 'Okay I suppose we can spend a little time, I'll tell the 'boys' to wait up, lets go' and so they ride back at speed towards the valley they had left that morning.

Richard has been calling to Roger but has received no answer, and he is not going to as he has been killed almost instantly by the shot which had hit his lungs and he has drowned in his own blood which poured from the wound and his mouth.

John is in a similar position, his mate David is still lying where he slumped to the ground and copious amounts of blood are beginning to stain the ground around him, John can't see any sign of life or movement and fears he has gone as well, and he can't get any response to his calls.

And so the two adversaries left remain about a 100 metres apart , John secure behind the wagon and Richard lying concealed in the Donga but wary of lifting his head for a further look and reconciled to the fact that Roger by now must be dead.

Richard decides his only opportunity will be to move away from the scene following the Donga until it appears to veer behind and to the North of the wagon, or further up the valley from where he may be able to shoot from cover and avenge his pal. Accordingly he retreats from his location and begins his move, meanwhile John is looking about trying to detect any movement as he doesn't know from what quarter any further move is going to come, but he does know that the other person out there isn't going to go away now and he wonders to himself 'who were those two? the only thing I can think of is that they are bounty hunters after the reward on our heads but if that's the case why didn't they just shoot us?

It is about an hour later when Louis and Bill re enter the valley and begin moving towards John hiding behind the wagon 'they must have heard the shots' he tells himself 'maybe I can bluff my way out of here'

' Hold up' he calls out 'we have been ambushed, must be rebels or deserters, they have attacked us and I think there's still one of them left somewhere, wait there and I will run towards you and we can figure out what to do' so saying he leaps to his feet and begins to run an erratic path towards them.

From behind him Richard rises to his feet, he has managed to stalk to within about 30 metres from where John was hiding and he raises his rifle and follows the lead as John runs towards the others and fires and watches as Richard falls shot in the back 'You there I surrender' he calls out to Louis and Bill 'don't shoot' but it s too late, they have seen the shot and fearing the worst have fired almost simultaneously and watch as Richard falls.

Louis and Bill walk around the scene, all of the participants are lying dead on the ground.

'What on Earth has happened here?' Bill asks as they are collecting the bodies and bringing them together by the shade of the wagon.

'My God, I think I know' calls out Louis ' this poor bugger we shot has got a reward notice in his pocket and its for those two Australians that spent the night with us, these two must have been bounty hunters and chasing then for the reward, I wonder why they didn't just shoot them out of hand from cover, there's another letter here we'll look at it shortly'

Elandsfontein

My Dearest Isabelle

Your brother and I have fallen upon some rotten luck.

We were on leave before we return to Canada and befriended a couple of chaps and were giving them a ride as they said they had been thrown off a train for no ticket.

Well so much for a bit of Christian reward because they set upon us and have stolen our money and possessions and left us tied up.

We have managed to escape and we relocated them in Wanderfontein and are about to follow them to get our money, horses and wagon back plus a reward that has been posted for them.

I will finish the letter when we return hopefully with good news.

'I thought I was finished with senseless killing and it looks like we have done for an innocent man' Bill cried out, 'God Damn it, he was trying to let us know but must have been so enraged with his mate being killed'

'Bill are you okay to wait here, I will go back and get some of the 'boys' and a wagon to take the bodies to Wanderfontein and with Bill's nod he begins to ride away.

It is after a time that Bill rises and walks around the area and notices the excavated material near a wheel of the old burnt out wagon and he kneels and begins to dig and within a few inches sights the Gold bars that have been buried there. 'That's what those two Australians were really after and that's why they called out -we might be back sooner than you think and rich- they weren't looking for somewhere to mine gold they knew of this stash and probably put it here!' he thought.

It was early that afternoon when Louis turned up with one of the wagons and a couple of the native boys, to be greeted by Bill 'come and see what I have found, explains a lot I think'

'I don't know what to do, I think this probably some of the Kruger reserves that we Boers were using to fund rifles and ammunition during the conflict and somehow those two have got it and hid it away until now' Louis explained. 'Right now we will load up the bodies and cover them with a tarpaulin and head away, between us we can both be rich and that's not even counting the reward for those two but I am not very happy about any of it, the poor chap we have shot was obviously innocent and after the reward and I feel bad about it, its okay killing people in a war, but not so good when you don't have to'

It is two days later when they call into the Constabulary at Wanderfontein and hand over the bodies to be given the reward.

Next day Bill is to entrain to Pretoria and then begin the long journey home to New Zealand and to resume his life and Louis is to search out a new client or use his share of the gold to purchase a farm and start again.

'Well Bill, its been my great pleasure, I never thought I could be friends with the enemy but its been good and even the 'boys' are going to miss you, you will be a rich man if you can get your share of the gold out of the country' Louis said. 'I sometimes wish there wasn't any of the bloody stuff in the world, its been the cause of the war, the loss of my great friend and his family and lots of heartache for my country and a lot of others as well as all the Mothers, Wives and Sweethearts'

Bill hailed a hansom cab 'Come with me for a last ride' he said to Louis and told the driver 'we want to go to the Mooi River Bridge and stop in the middle', when they pulled to a stop Bill walked to the edge of the bridge unbuckling his travel bag 'I feel like you about this stuff, there's been too much killing and the final straw was us taking away the life of that poor Canadian, due to get married and we cut his life short, but I also recall that poor Marie and all the others in those camps, one day someone else can get rich with another gold strike but its already been smelted in to ingots for him' and he reached into his bag and threw the gold into the river below.

'Wait for me, ah to hell with it I guess I can live without it too, I have a hundred pounds extra, the 'boys' can have half for a bonus and I have enough to outfit another hunting safari' and Louis threw his gold into the river as well.

And so ended Louis and Bill's war and as they drove away each to his own new life Bill said 'At least you and I have something special to tell our Grandchildren one day, how we went from being rich in about 30 seconds back to nothing special but at least we can hold our heads up!'

THE END

Made in the USA
Columbia, SC
06 October 2020

22155690R00079